White Moon

White Moon

Mehreen Ahmed

Bridge House

British Library Cataloguing in Publication Data
A Record of this Publication is available from the British
Library

ISBN 978-1-914199-90-5

This edition published 2025 by Bridge House Publishing
Manchester, England

This book is dedicated to my mother, Mrs. Sarwari Alam, and my father Mr. Manzur Alam, whose voracious readings and relentless support have been paramount.

Contents

Preface

White Moon is a collection of avant-garde short stories, micro and flash fiction. All of the incidents in this book depict imaginary characters and events underpinned by dreamlike, strong surrealistic, even esoteric connections. The narratives bring together a unique blend of absorbing, entertaining and otherworldly experience.

Sensible Shoes

I sat here, like a loyal friend, by her floor bed. Waiting for my owner, Samira Khan, to wake up. She did in a while. I saw her frowning and looking groggy. Lying on her pillow, she reached out for a wooden box which held her medication. Last night, like every other night, she'd filled up her small pitcher and placed it beside her bed. She took out a pill blister pack, pinched one out, and popped it into her mouth. She swallowed hard with some water from the pitcher. With a sigh of relief, she lay back on the pillow. She looked vaguely at a pair of pants hanging from a hook on the bedroom door – not hers. The morning was dull and dreary with deep, hanging clouds. She pushed and rolled herself out.

A vegetable vendor was shouting on the street. Just as well, I also heard his croaky voice and readied myself. Samira was going to run downstairs. He always came along with his cart at this time of the day. My owner slid her feet and rested them roughly upon my tongue. She checked her vegetable basket, and realised that she was out of potatoes and green papaya. She craned her neck through the window and told him to pack her one kilo of potatoes and one medium sized papaya. Quickly, she picked up her purse and climbed down the stairs. On the street, the vendor had wrapped her potatoes and green papaya in an old, crumpled newspaper sheet. Samira opened her purse and gave him the money for a kilo of potato and a green papaya. The vendor took the notes with a polite smile, but said that the price had gone up because of inflation.

"Since when?" Samira asked.

I listened.

"There's an inflation, didn't you know? It was in the news?"

11

"I know. High electricity bills, petrol price hike, and what have you? How much?"

The price had doubled. Samira frowned and looked into her purse. There was no money left.

"Stay here; I'll have to go upstairs to fetch the extra some."

"Okay. Please don't be late. Time is money. I got a family of five to feed."

"I know."

Samira smiled and left as he hung around in the dull street. She went upstairs and searched for money. She went through all her purses, scrambling for coins and loose notes here and there. She gathered them in a rush and sat down to count them. It was barely enough. She took it all and raced downstairs to the waiting vendor. She gave him all she had. Mad, she had the right amount – somehow. As she turned around, I felt a pressure pain and I caved in a little long.

"Uff," I uttered.

Thumbing her temples, she slowly came back up the stairs. She would have to get dressed in an hour to go to work. The bus stand, thankfully, was not far. She went straight into the kitchen, grabbed a peeler off the rack and began to peel the potatoes and the green papaya. She mixed it with turmeric, red chillies, oil, and a dash of salt. Turning on the stove, she placed the pot and reduced the heat. While it cooked in the gentle flame, she went into the bathroom to take a bucket bath. Her feet released me. I felt relieved.

A few mugs of pail water down her back; after the bath, she dried herself with a towel and put on a cotton sari, combing her long black hair. She added some lipstick to her pale lips. The curried potatoes and the green papaya were cooked by now. She sat down in bare feet to have her meal in the kitchen with a couple of dry, hard chapatis left overnight. There was no time to make tea. She washed her hands, picked up her purse, and slid her feet into me. Off she climbed down the stairs again. On the street, she hurried towards the bus stop. But her bus had stopped and left: she was late. Her jaw fell. She called a passing rickshaw and got on it. I felt rested. Just then, she realised that she didn't have enough money to pay him. Which meant she would have to borrow from a colleague once she reached her office? Unless she went into her bank first. She asked the rickshaw to stop in front of the bank. She told him to wait here. The man wiped off his sweat with a soft towel around his neck and inclined against the passenger seat where she had been sitting. Samira crossed the street. I was her sturdiest, best pair of sandals she ever had, which she had been wearing for donkey's years. She crossed the street and entered the bank. A quarter of an hour passed, she returned. Her rickshaw was still there.

She was a good Samaritan. At the office, she not only paid fare to the rickshaw-puller but also some extra tip because she had made him wait. The man took it happily: not everyone was fair. Most people haggled. But Samira didn't, not even with the vendor this morning. She walked over five high steps, dipping her weight duly into me and entering the office building where she worked as a secretary. It was awfully noisy today. What was wrong? She asked a colleague. The colleague replied that the company was folding. They were all out of jobs.

What? Out of job meant no pay. She saw how the other girls were behaving. Some screamed, some even fainted. Others sobbed silently. She dug her toes deeper into me. She offered them no consolation; soberly, she watched them despair. This level-headed person – my owner – chose me as her sensible sandals. In all the world, I could never fail her, nor cause her to break a bone or cause her to lead an invalid life by tripping her over. Such a long journey she walked in me, while I had her back all along: I didn't fall apart. I knew that she felt strangely secure with me – her trusted sandals.

Samira thought of bootstrapping as an alternative mode. Typically, the vendors were the real battlers of struggle streets: they were her real heroes. They grew and sold their own vegetables. In her view, they never made boots for the kings. Samira decided to strap her boots and invest in a start-up business. She thought of selling jewellery. She took out money from the deep pockets of the pants hanging on her door. She bought jewellery from craftsmen and decided to sell it in a shop. She needed to find a shop. I took her on paths, she never thought of traveling – to walk her walks. Without wasting any time, I took her to a developer. She asked them if she could rent a shop in their newly-built, glamorous building. They promised her one. They said she could. On that promise, Samira went ahead to a jeweller and made a deposit of 20%. In one short month, she picked up the jewellery and had a whole load to start her business with. However, when she went back to her developers, they told her that the new shop wasn't available for rent. This was a setback. It disappointed her. She asked, "Why not?" They told her, because unless all the other new shops were tenanted, she couldn't have hers.

"What? What a crazy idea? You are breaking your promise."

"Well, it's just a promise. No legal paperwork was in place."

Samira realised that without a shop all she had was this beautiful dream. Still, she had me. I took her back to the same developers. She asked them to help her out. They told her she could rent a kiosk, instead. Samira agreed straightaway. Although she would have preferred a shop, if she had this kiosk, she could at least sell her dream. Every morning, Samira walked to the kiosk, sat there long summer days into sunsets. It wasn't easy at first, like everything else, nothing was really easy. But my soles had not yet disintegrated. They remained sturdy – a friend by her side, rain or sunshine. I took her places where her dream could become a reality.

Sure, the kiosk wasn't the best option. But the market was changeable, too. And she also wasn't going anywhere anytime soon. This, her meal ticket, was as real as the cart was to the vendor, and the rickshaw to the puller. Days went by, months and then a whole new year had gone. Samira sold a lot. She bought and she sold. After about a year and a half, the developer came to her and offered her the shop she had desired. She couldn't believe this. In those same loyal sandals – me – she moved her trinket boxes to the shell of the shop which was now going to house her big dream – all done. I did my diligent miles – the dirt and the grime were now hard-pressed on my tongue, mapped out a grim, grimy destiny of strife.

Then one night, Samira came home late. She took me off and placed me in my usual place by the bed. She curled up under the blanket. I shivered and sentineled. When she woke up the next morning, she didn't look at me even once. Neither were those familiar male pants hanging here anymore. I realised my days were numbered. Where was I? I was right there, where she put me every night. I had done my hard work, bore the brunt of it all without a hitch like a silent sole "scream" painting on a wall. I flew her out on her whimsical air; the promised shop or not, her sandals were I, worn out but undeterred. Who took a whole gamut of the idiosyncratic business world in my stride? My tracks marked a solitary, but a solid pathway – she was successful. Just as those pants were gone, I was made redundant too, without any consequence to her. I heard her suppress a

15

giggle and mumble, "Funny, this love? You have to have the looks too for me or anyone to love you so?"

Old shoes, she cast me aside like a pair of disposables. Flat on my face, I saw that she took out another expensive pair from a shoe box. She despised the idea of making boots for the kings. Really? In those new shoes, she'd be doing just that. I was morose – someone else's pants hung on the door.

_____

Originally published in *Litro Magazine,* UK, April 2023

Water Hyacinth

Amir stops saying hello in a while. The last time we spoke, he was complaining. The little shack where he lives has a leaky roof; the water has to be contained in buckets, pots, and pans placed around under every leak. I haven't seen anything like it. I asked him to fix the leaks. He smiled and he pointed his left hand towards an empty clay stove at the far end of the shack without a word. Otherwise, I thought the room was pretty spacious, four-cornered, not triangular or rectangular. Amir isn't deaf-mute, however, not much of a talker either. Days go by sometimes without him uttering even a word apart from just a grimace or body language talk.

I haven't seen him in weeks. Today, I want to stop by his shack. He lives alone as far as I can tell from the few times I visited him. I walk up to his room this morning but find that the door is shut. I knock. No one responds. I gingerly push it with my index finger. Sunlight pours into the dark room. The pots and pans are all here under each leak, but no Amir anywhere.

He may have gone to the toilets, or perhaps to work. Standing alone for some time in the middle of the room, and feeling a bit lost, I crane my neck to see some photos on the terracotta walls which eluded me that first time I visited here. These are kitsch, images of women posed from various garish angles, cut-outs, and pasted over the cracks with cheap glue.

Why do I even care so much for Amir? I wonder. Who the hell is he anyway? Does it really matter who he is or where he is from? But for some reason, I can't bring myself to ignore him either. I'm convinced that there is more to him. Which elude me? I have only just skimmed the surface.

He works as a *bawarchee* – a chef in Kitchen Corner Hotel on Shayaam Bazaar Road in old Dhaka. His specialty is *morog biriyani* among other things, and sweets such as *shahi tukra* make the tongue salivate just by thinking about them. It's a booming business, and the first time I meet him is as a customer, waiting with a number between my fingers, given to me at the entrance by a teaboy. In the long queue I stand patiently to place my order. He sees me and takes a shine to me. Is it my clothes, the patched up jeans and a snow white tea shirt that I am wearing? He calls out my number, number 13. I realise it is my turn. I place the order as he winks at me and asks where I bought those jeans. Did I buy them locally or abroad? He is so taken by my jeans that it makes me wonder about his fashion tastes. Just a *bawarchee*! He gives me an extra serve of *morog biriyani*, on the house too.

We start talking when he comes by and sits at my table. "Time and time again, timelessly, and tirelessly, I tell people the same story of a short-lived life."

"How so?" I ask.

"Where do you live?" he asks me.

"Just down the alley."

"The marble mansion?"

I look at him and then at my plate of biryani-flavoured hot meal before me.

"Well? Is it that house or not?" he asks again.

I nod slightly and begin to eat. He stands up with some alacrity saying something like, "when a person dies the living cry, not the dead, the dead can't cry." He leaves me reeling from whatever the saying may allude to: passage of time, or is it something else? I quickly finish my meal. On my way out, I look for the chef, but I can't see him anywhere. I think I want to visit him at his place, but he has disappeared before I can even get his address. I ask one of his staff if he knows.

He sure does; it does not take much coaxing either to get it out him. All I do is utter the magic phrase of my residence, the great mansion down the road – open sesame, the address comes out of his mouth like rote learning.

My grandfather and his father had a powerful hold over the alley. They wanted to be legends, they became so. So much so that even after their deaths, many years later when my generation grew up, I inherited the mansion's spirit. I am also an inheritor of amassed wealth. Wherever I go, I carry the mansion's bad name like a dark shadow. The fact that I am not like them, that I try to rehash the ill repute and repudiate the evils associated with it, is ignored by society at large; not a soul understands. The mansion stinks like a skunk on the pages of history.

In the heart of it, I traverse the top deck of a multi-levelled ship, sunbathing every day in the fresh new light. Just a deck below is a dark, musty hall full of people who are traveling too alongside, except these are third-class people who cannot afford the sunny deck above. Living on the fringe, trying to push through the boundaries in vain to be on top, and walk as an equal with the others. A few lucky ones may make it, but others continue to fight tooth and nail to no avail.

No matter the top deck or the bottom, as the ship sails, so does everyone onboard. Even though it may seem like some of the lower-deck people are stuck in a weird time warp stopping them from being upwardly mobile. Imagine the eternal drudgery of unfulfilled dreams: Amir's envy drilling a hole in his heart so big that no amount of success as a chef can fill it up! He can never make it to the mansion.

What does he want? Is he even mansion material? I have to return to find out, and befriend him. Find out how deep is his desire to become a mansion master. My quest is purely journalistic. But I also want to point out a recourse to stop his internal bleeding. Like a fairy tale palace, the mansion overwhelms his senses; they foretell danger from a wild king whose cannibalistic domination rules over the valley – both awe-inspiring and frightening to the residents on the lower plains of the alley, commoners such as Amir, in the mansion's shadowy presence, his every effort fails before the towering success of the mansion people.

Impossible. I can't find Amir anywhere in or around his house nor in his restaurant. His staff are also clueless. The last time we met was just over a week ago. He was standing in the pouring rain waiting for a bus. I joined him and tried to squeeze under his umbrella which he shared reluctantly.

"Why are you here?" he asked.

"I want to chat with you."

"What about?" his voice quivered.

"I can't tell you in this rain, let's go somewhere dry."

"Dry?" he laughed. "I can't think of any other place higher and dryer than your hilltop mansion."

"No, I mean somewhere, anywhere other than the mansion."

"Well, you'd better come to my shack then. Would you be dry enough there?" he asked with a wink.

I pretended not to get drawn into the sarcasm. I said bluntly, "Yes."

"Okay."

Amir and I walked through the zigzag water puddles on the narrow dirt road. The winding road finally ended at the shack. We stepped under a protruded roof. Amir shook off the water from the umbrella and closed it. Opening the door, he bade me in to sit on a high-backed chair beside a plank bed, on the edge of which he sat tentatively looking at me. I knew he was trying to fathom the unfathomable of the "whys".

"What's with you and the mansion?" I asked.

My directness didn't seem to puzzle him. He appeared calm.

"The taxes, the bullying, the subjugation, don't tell me you don't already know."

"I know that taxes have been raised recently and people have been protesting and have been thrown into the dungeon."

"Then, why do you ask?"

"Any other curiosities?" I asked.

"Are you kidding me? Isn't this enough? Say, what is your name?"

"My name is Monsur Ali Khawaja, nephew to the current *Dewaan*."

"Nephew to the King?" he smirked. "So, has your uncle pissed you off or something that you have now come here to befriend a commoner?"

"No, not at all. I am here to put you in my shoes, and me in yours."

"That's silly. Why would you do that? It doesn't make any sense."

"It makes perfect sense to me. I would like to walk you through the mansion, the dungeon and all."

"What makes you think I want it?"

"Your eyes."

"Really? That obvious?"

I smiled. "Well, what do you say?"

He took time to think for a while and then he said sheepishly, "OK, but what do you want in return?"

"Your rags," I said.

"Seriously?" he asked.

"Yep, seriously."

"Would these pants and shirt do? Or do I need to get changed in case I meet the *Dewaan*?" he asked.

"Nope."

He stood up and followed me out. We took off to the mansion up the alley in Shayaam Bazaar Road in Dhaka where his restaurant was also situated. We walked together down the alley, but his restaurant wasn't there. People were clothed differently in loincloths sarongs and bare chests. Wealthy people were clad in gold, top to toe. Beautiful women's bare breasts were also clad in gold chain layers of necklaces. Amir, who was beside me was dressed in rich people's clothes. I was clad in rags. My sandals were torn, his weren't, but they were brawny enough, moulded in slush, syrupy gold.

A horse stood at a distance from us under an age-old banyan. Amir looked at me, smiled, and whistled at the horse. It galloped and stopped in front of him to mount, while I walked up the hills where the mansion was. At the mansion gate, guards stood with staff weapons. As soon as they saw Amir, they bowed and let us both in. Inside the mansion murals of goddesses decked the palace walls and pillars distinctive of a Kamrupa Kingdom; its long stretch from Assam through the southern boundary to the River Brahmaputra, where gathered water hyacinth floated unhindered up and downstream along the river. Who cared about their origin?

Amir vanished. Where was I? Where was Amir? Who was Amir? I found myself walking through this palace of a Kamrupa King which was not my mansion – my residence, at all. It was all theirs. And Amir? I stepped into the throne room; I saw him crowned as an ancient king. Amir looked at me quizzically and clapped to call his personal guards to arrest me and have me thrown into the dungeon for trespassing. I even saw a diabolic grin wavering on his dark cupid lips. Really? I swore under my breath. This was not him. He was someone else, he was a *Pushyabhuti* coined in a 7th century bronze and copper currency. Echoing within the sooty, old walls of the narrow, dark corridor, I heard a rhyme fading. I turned my head around and saw a girl gazing at me. She was standing behind Amir's throne wearing a flashing armour and holding a gleaming wand. I couldn't see her anymore. She took off, whiffed away in a cloud of smoke as though she didn't even have a bodily existence – this, a figment from the past Amir had lived through all those years, the past had dissipated at a mere swish of the wand. She whispered her name to me – Kanta Karnavati.

Back in the day, growing up I played with a little girl who looked exactly like her – a ditto face cut-out. She was our neighbour's daughter who belonged to a house of black cats. I used to call her Luna because she had captivating, ember cat eyes.

I blinked, and it was all gone as though it never existed. Magic, it sure was, the past and the present were fused into my mind. I walked past a picture window in Amir's palace and watched dappled lights in the garden of another day. Amir was King, a *Pushyabhuti*, this time around. The nursery rhymes anchored the past into my memory of an undeniable, underwater sinkhole. The past, the present, and the future in the human narrative of a timeline, floated like water hyacinth.

Back in my old clothes, I walk down the alley carefree, I view people milling about in Amir's restaurant like scattered ants, queueing up for a great meal of *morog biriyani*. The mansion is right behind me, here and now, a century-old solid rock. I walk up to the restaurant and join the long queue. I see a blackhead bobbing in the crowd, Chef Amir

23

serving in the restaurant. He looks almost content. He sees me and winks. We are talking again.

———————————

First published in *Panorama: The Journal of Travel, Place, and Nature,* UK, November 2023

Dappled Lights

Two women sat on the brink of a Long River at sunset. One had a salt and pepper mane, the other a shaved head. The salt and pepper haired woman held a red lantern. She pressed her lips until her cheeks dimpled. Her pupils darted over the rippled waves. Her eyes appeared dull and teary, eye bags sagged underneath. She had a bulging pouch on her lap tied up in double knots to its middle top. The first two knots were tied out of two ends of a square loincloth forming rectangles; the remaining end rectangles of the cloth were knotted over the first two knots. Boats arrived and left. She didn't get on in any of them. She yawned, but she was lucid as she communicated with the shaved head. The shaved head woman nodded. Salt and pepper took out a water bottle from her pouch, and offered it to her. Leaning against the great banyan, she then spaced out.

A sprightly teenager, she was a dancer in the academy of the fine arts. Her dance steps were as nuanced, as she was poised. The centre stage scented the lily perfume she wore in rich profusion. Her mane was dense monsoon rain, long and flowing down her slender waist. Her fame spread a fair bit into the wen. That people could smell her lily-odoured body, even as they breathed, heard her anklets ring, and felt her delicate moves when they dreamed. Whom she allowed to be close, and whom she didn't, all hinged on her mood.

A certain man then came along one evening, she was dancing on the floor, the man entered and unlike all other men, boldly crossed the floor and held her hands. He too began to dance with her following her intricate choreograph. Naive as he was, she took it upon herself to teach him all; taught him how to dance, forever they shall dance. In her beating heart, dance reigned supreme; it melted any walls. They stepped outside the dance court into The Garden of Love and Delight. Entwined like vines, they danced as she unlocked the secrets of her arts to him; the dance which had been locked in her heart. This garden was their shrine.

She felt replete; she realised she had been incomplete. By far, her reality had been a confusing blur until now, a deficiency which had barred truth from entering, had it not been for him. The duo danced in the dappled lights in The Garden of Love and Delight; within the shrubbery, boughs and the vines, broad, aged leaves of the banyan trees, whose twisted knots made for a sturdier dancing plain. The duo danced till the glowing lights of the Sirius, the bright Dog Star, illuminated the night sky.

One night, however, since day and night were equal to the dancers, who had lost count of time through countless encounters, without tomorrows or yesterdays or todays anytime, one day she made herself unavailable for the schooling of this young man. She neither appeared in the court, nor into the garden, but made him wait until he departed, despondent without understanding what had happened to her overnight, had she been in an accident? Looming dark clouds gathered in the ceaseless sky; a storm was coming on; thunder cracked the firmament.

Still, he hadn't given up hope; the young man had a dull thought; perhaps she hadn't come because she couldn't. Perhaps, she got held up in the storm, which was about to start soon. As the day progressed, all dreary and white, wherever she was, his groins groaned, as did all of his body parts ache, including his soul. In the thick of it, the plot thickened. At midnight through many harrowing plights, the young man came and went away in vain as the mistress never came, such a shame that she was not even in his dream. Until now, he was able to remain steadfast, but not any more. His pain grew, no more than he was restive. This academy had become a barren place.

It soon came to pass that the mistress had disappeared without a trace, as though she had dissipated. She wasn't seen on the dance floor any more; when he'd peeked through the open door one night, there was another young dancer, who looked at him through the corner of her keen kohl eyes. He wasn't mesmerised. Enticing as she was, when her seductive glances failed, he wondered why this had happened. What had happened to the pleasures of his flesh, why could he not be aroused by this new enchantress? She approached him in person and took his hands in hers.

She led him into her own bed-chamber of brick and mortar, away from the besotted Garden of Love and Delight. The severance from his own mistress formed shards of glass bruise, made this a cold place, a cold case; walls were closing in; he felt claustrophobic; it betrayed an emotion. Here, Kohl tried to pick up the pieces, to piece him in. Why was it futile? Why had she failed? Kohl asked. Was she any less in the art? He returned a smile and said he needed to retune himself to the new tunes, readjust his moves, if only he could, none of it was her fault. She must dance along with or without him.

A moment of self-realisation, his own mistress had once taught him, only too perfectly in tune with nature that his flesh had absorbed it all. Kohl looked at him, bemused, what school of philosophy was he in? Why was his young heart so hard like the chhurpi aged cheese? She understood nothing of it, and retreated into her chamber with a frown of reproach which the young man saw but scratched his beard to leave her to her flutters and moans. He had embarked on a different path to seek out his elusive mistress; smitten by her, he would wait it out; a lifetime of waiting, maybe, he resolved. Maybe, it was all his fault; a scathed self-criticism unveiled a deluded notion.

Godot had waited. He did too, like him he waited for the phantom, the woman who never returned. Who owed it to him, to own up for what she did, who vowed under a white noon moon, never to leave any time soon. Why had she become a Godot phantom? Or Lilith, perhaps? He, a sea-farer, was going to return to the seas after all, at some turning point of the waves, or travel to another port where he would dock his ship, hence Lilith decided to rebel and leave? Albeit, the dance was flash; in a flash, it had fleshed out onto the esoteric realm. Such was the nature of their dance – in the moment, it had mediated through the body and reached a zenith into the souls; her anklet bells chimed an undying finesse.

The body and the soul went hand in hand, philosophy of religion, as Aristotle held. In its intrinsic oneness, the body couldn't function without its soul. Bereaved, his own soul had broken down, starved, long gone. The academy had mirrored such flashes of self-realisations, that these dances were well beyond the physical expressions. The beaches were lonely, oyster shells lay bare, amassed and garnered strength along the coastline like a garland of growing void etched in his heart. He could have had anyone. Sailors had a wife at every port, the cliché goes.

Tides were tied with time. Just as tired, the ship was bound to their flips of tiered motions. He used this time well. He used the seas to look for the phantom, and to try to turn the tides around. But glad tidings awaited still, scarce, he braced himself for the worst as he continued to search. Was she just plainly fanciful, chiding, or seriously dancing with him? His heart was brimming with many questions, and with many quiet expectations. Still, she was close by, her breathing was intense upon him, the winds sprayed the sultry smell of the sea; swelling waves crept in and cringed out on the ocean shore, he heard her lulling a moonlight lore, as though, she still protected him and tried to preserve this rare dance of sanctity. Or was it all a fallacy?

He persevered. It was a virtue. Was she even beautiful? While they were engaged in the dance, he had not noticed enough to see through. He beheld beauty when he saw her chiselled, dimpled cheeks framed within the delicate bones of her face. Her face shone every time he closed his eyes now, her sighs into his ears. He danced a tango with her. He smelt her scents. Her crooked dance fingers dug into the porous skin of his neck, beauty was only skin-deep, her allure, and her unfailing wisdom cut the insides of his turgid heart, he heard her sweet callings, her raw moans he heard them as fresh as yesterday, to which he responded with a slight, "oou?" Until his hammock swung in the misty ocean brew.

There was a clue. Words had speared through the wild night why the enchantress had disappeared; he was spared, drunk in sorrow they hadn't caught his ears. He thought he was all ears. An unnamed merchant had asked her favours to teach him about the art, who wanted her as a flavour of the month to which she had refused, because she already had a partner, the one she had favoured.

But the merchant was livid. He made an extraordinary threat. He strode across the dance floor and ordained that he would behead her if she continued in The Garden of Love and Delight with another man; that he would behead the man too. She wouldn't fawn him, but fled like one to lie still into the dark so she couldn't be found. She escaped to the southern fringe of the city by the Long River to live in solitude with her mother who had enrolled her here as a child to learn the ropes, and the arts.

She wasn't just a nameless educator. She had a name that she went by in the academy. Her name was Nirmala. The young man's name was Siddhartha. She didn't have the courage to tell him, because she feared the wealthy merchant, a powerful man, would come after him and have them both beheaded. Instead, Nirmala started a calm life in hiding with her mother. But every morning she walked up to the river and moped for Siddhartha, hoping for a reunion.

Her mother was blind. But a seer in blindness, she noted that a page had been turned in her daughter's life. A flower had blossomed in her heart as she doted on a man. She felt her profound sorrow. One day, however, she heard Nirmala throwing up. She perceived the nature of the malady for it was a sweet love child she carried. With little to eat, her mother asked Nirmala to find work for the sake of the child, at least. Nirmala wasn't showing at that stage. She found work on a farm, not too far from where they had lived. This farm grew poppies, mace and nutmeg where Nirmala's job was to crush the mace and the nutmeg. The resin from the nutmeg often clouded her breathing space. The poisonous powder gave her dizzy spells.

After weeks of hard toil at grinding, inhaling the nutty, mace powder in a mortar, one evening before sun-set Nirmala lost consciousness. An on-duty supervisor tried to wake her up but she couldn't, so the employer had to be notified, who wrote back giving instructions of her sack. His reasons were too simplistic, that she was unfit for work. Why else would she faint? But she recovered. Nirmala found herself out of a job. Determined to get her job back, she wanted to meet the big boss. Here was a situation. Unfair, it sure was to relieve her from her duties. She asked the supervisor to arrange a meeting. After much deliberation she agreed, and a meeting date was fixed on the Monday week.

This day, Nirmala decided to dress to kill. She wore her

best costume and jewellery to impress him. She knew this would work. She was exceptional. However, she didn't know who her boss was. She put on her magic lily perfume which her mother could smell. She could also hear the anklet bells; she feared the worst. She fumbled through the door to ask. Nirmala sprung a surprise and told her what had happened at work. That she was meeting the big boss to get her job back. Which was why she was dressing up to conceal her pregnancy. However, her mother told her that this wouldn't fare well. With a sense of foreboding, she forbade her to meet him but to look for work in another place.

Work was hard to find, and being a court dancer, Nirmala had even fewer options. Looking at herself today, she knew that her job was going to be reinstated. She was tempting fate. Her mother panicked and advised Nirmala against it. But she paid no heed. Clad in gold jewellery she had from her dancing days, she looked stunning like she always did, when men lay at her feet. She had also tucked something else in her clothing. Nirmala hid a small *kukri*, inside the *nivi*, the top fold of her body, should the boss's behaviour turn sour and unworthy. She hoped for the best outcome although she didn't know his true intent. Who was he anyway? She never met him, just the supervisors these fine days over at her job stay. Mace power was sprayed in the air from grinding, she hadn't strayed, she still had some self-respect left.

She kissed her mother's forehead, and asked her to kiss her back on her dimples. Nirmala took a deep breath and stepped outside into the open. She walked towards the mace farm in her white loincloth. A single garb costume, wrapped around her shoulders and waist and extended around her two legs, was belted with a gold waistband across her underbelly of an exposed satiny midriff. On her way, she plucked a

31

fragile white lily from a roadside tree, and slipped it into the masses of her tightly plaited tresses. Her fair skin looked translucent, her classical nose dazzled a diamond stud; gold conch-shell for earrings, matched the golden anklets and the intricate bracelets, the gold band around her forehead. What people wouldn't pay, and pray to be with her? She fell prey to a vile merchant's foul play.

He played her. But she had her nose in the air, she proceeded towards the farm, and stepped up as she neared it. She swaggered as she paced. Had she not fainted, she would have made it to the top? Faint-hearted she was not. If she made it as an enchantress in her court, then she could make it here too, as priestess of nutmeg crushing load. This was a different kind of a dance to switch into, this new dance mode. Her life went awry. Siddhartha's child made her wary. She felt weary. He was chasms away, and she couldn't dance in her court. She was never a trout; a potent cocktail mix of the merchant's threat pulled her into jeopardy – The Garden of Love and Delight, once full of unspoken pledge had become a place of discontent.

One step at a time. Her nimble feet wore the red alta dye. She proceeded towards the gated mansion where her employer waited to meet her this clear day. A slight autumnal breeze murmured a tune and blew some curly locks across her fine facial bones, the guards opened the gates. She entered and walked along the way, such a long walk, where his mansion stood at the end of this peat path. A maid let her in through solid mahogany doors. She led her down a mosaic corridor, dimly lit into a room of many ornamental sofas and high-backed chairs where yet another door, a door within a door, within a door bridged this long wormhole of a corridor.

At last, the last door opened. She stood on its precipice,

and saw a man standing several steps below, a wine glass in hand. She was ushered in by the maid; the maid left rapidly. She was hemmed in on all sides, all doors slammed. She climbed down the long staircase, shortly. He turned around. She was astounded by whom she saw, too late. Who else, but the formidable merchant, who had caused her so much distress. She stood rooted to the floor petrified in her mind and banged her head hundred times for not listening to her mother who had cautioned her. She tried to turn around to flee.

Fight or flight. The villain squinted and gasped, "You? Is this really who I think it is?" He strode towards her, and looked straight into her long lashed eyes. He smiled with a twinkle of victory in his own, while beads of sweat emerged on her upper lips. He slid a finger down her bare shoulders. His grasping ten, dug into her velvet arms; he pulled her closer while she trembled with fear. Of course, he was willing to give her a job, but not the job of a crusher of the nutmeg and the mace, but to fan a fantasy he had been gnawing at all along. She'd gone missing. Now she was here, right under his nose with all the doors closed.

The thought of the child knocked her back to cognisance. Transience of all things on earth as her dance with Siddhartha, but, but meaningful. She thought of it, as she fought her angry tears for not listening to her seer mother. She knew she had the *kukri*, but her reason prevailed. That killing this man would only bring more danger, inevitable jail, possibly the gallows. She tried to negotiate.

"Could I have my old job back, please?"

Even she thought she sounded naive.

He laughed. "What I'm about to offer you is much, much worthy of you? All this? All this could be yours if you taught me to dance, and made me slave and student to your nuance."

"I could do this no more than you could grind your own mace. I'm with child," she said.

"I remember why you shunned me at the academy. I had vowed to behead you if you didn't submit."

"I beg you. I still can't. I carry a baby inside of me."

"Then I shall imprison you at once. I don't care about the baby you carry in that impure womb of yours."

No more than a sugar daddy, that was his proposed offer? Her hand fumbled through the folds of her clothing as it reached down for the *kukri*, she took it out and lunged straight into his eyes in frenzy, she punctured one of his eyeballs, until the man's vision blurred, he screamed in agony. A pool of blood was formed on the mosaic floor behind all the sound proof doors.

Done. Blood was on her hands too, she hid the *kukri* under her layered clothing, running up the stairs, flung open the doors, one after another running along the corridor. None but his own doing, she staggered and stumbled, and made her way through this fluid wormhole. Back on the peat path, the guards were having tea and a few chats, while she unlatched a small gate. They didn't notice. She slipped through it.

She entered her hut; she was befuddled. She asked her mother to pack a cotton pouch because they would have to leave as soon as possible. Thankfully, the merchant was blind only in the one eye; he had not died. But the sore eye was enough to pour sour into their lives. The situation was grave; it behoved her to save this baby and her mother. This merchant whose long hands, she feared, could grab her from any four corners of the world, but she had to take her chances and had taken a bold step forward.

She led her mother to the edge of the Long River. Beneath a yellow *bindi* sky, they waited for a boat. In this short while, they could hear scuffles behind a tree. The full moon shed some light on men who entered the empty hut shell. Darkness wrapped Nirmala and her mother, who lay low in the dirt path of the bank masking themselves with soft mud in the semblance of a camouflage.

The men came as far as the river bank; they even looked down, but all they could see was mud and a murky water body stretched far out with the moonbeam frolicking. Nirmala and her mother were right there, under the feet of those men, hiding down in a black hole as it were. The fair enchantress was covered in muck, as was her mother to whom the night's darkness meant nothing much, however, who saw this coming all along; her undiminished sight.

A boat came by like an apparition through the dark, a skeletal boatman boned at the helm. He took them on board and oared away. He rowed his boat until the morning's first dew dropped on the grass blades. While the merchant was ramping up violence, setting the hut ablaze, the smoke was high up in the sky. The last thing they saw, they knew, had to be their own hut. By now, a banyan tree was sighted along the Long River, where the boatman oared them up to the shore and secured the boat for his passengers to get off, still covered in dirt. He couldn't see their faces at all on which the mud had dried. They jumped off the boat with a thud, the maiden took her ring off and paid the boatman, who was too happy to receive real gold; the treat was rare.

On the shore, the mother and the daughter treaded slowly. They knew not where to go, so they walked on until they found a shack where some tea was brewing in a pot, a tea boy stood with a tall and lanky man. When they approached them, the boy was frightened to see their faces and bodies well covered in cracky mud. The mother and the daughter needed to rest; however, this was no resting place. The man offered to take them to his house which was close by so they could wash-up, rest and be fed. From here they could decide their journey's next leg. He asked them to wash in the river, then return, while he prepared breakfast.

Nirmala washed her mother first, then herself. She took all her jewellery off, one piece after another and put them in the cotton pouch which carried their clothes and some bric-à-brac. Her mother told her to give the man some jewellery in lieu of his kindness if he would let them stay, as he didn't seem to have a family of his own; they could be his family, cook and clean for him while Nirmala had her baby.

The man heard the unabridged tale of the vile merchant's chants. It was a grisly story of terror and of tragedy. He offered them solace and his home; he felt nothing but sorrow for them. Such an offer they also couldn't turn down. On life's unpredictability, Nirmala felt her luck was turning; her baby was growing through all trimesters.

One August evening, as they had just sat down to have dinner, she went into labour. The man rushed out to find his neighbour, whose midwifery delivered a strong baby boy. The man told his neighbours that the baby's father had passed away, she was his niece, her mother, a step-sister had come to take refuge here because of misfortunes elsewhere. Their hut had burned down. That plausible story stuck. More misfortunes lay in the offing, yet. Nirmala's beauty could not be blighted. The neighbourhood men ogled at her, whetting a desire. She knew they had an appetite for her. Too afraid, she was clueless as to how to shew them; as if they were crows, as if they were going to go away. Since no one aided, these men inched in closer, but she also had a baby, and was a lactating mother.

One day, a young man proposed to her that he wanted to marry her, but, without the baby, her blind mother could raise it in this very house. Nirmala found his proposal outrageous. She said, "no" straightaway. The man went away seething in anger but hatched a terrible plan. He kidnapped the baby from the napping mother in the fading light on an August day. When she woke up, she couldn't find her baby anywhere. Madly, looking for him everywhere, mostly along the riverside, she intuited, until she heard a cry which was coming from a boat nearby. Nirmala followed the cry and ran to the boat; she found her child in another woman's lap, who had bought the baby from a kidnapper's sack.

"My baby is not for sale," she screamed and she snatched it from her lap. In return, she gave the woman her only diamond nose-stud, far more expensive than money could buy. The woman grabbed it and returned the baby. Nirmala's joy was boundless. Life's ever bumpy roads, she set foot in a crossroads, and wondered which way her Siddhartha went. The Long River laid many dead bodies. Her baby's kidnapper was also one amongst them. Who killed him and why was unknown, but the police search was on as they marched into every home. This created an impediment for all other men, Nirmala's suitors, who were frightened and did not dare leave their dens.

With each day, her burning beauty slowly waned; she was aging and aging fast. The boy was growing up, looking more and more like Siddhartha. The enchantress, once renowned for her performance, on whom countless doted, bestowed honour, while she only melded with one. Her fair complexion was several notches paler, she had less appetite, and her taut body slowly loosened.

Many years had passed. Her boy was now fifteen. Her blind mother died on a moonless night. She had a river burial in the same Long River. Her son, a rising sun. Never in limbo, she knew, one day her Siddhartha would return, no matter how ugly she had become; she had taught him a sublime dance in The Garden of Love and Delight, and he would remain untarnished. Before her mother died, the seer saw in her future that he would return. When that might happen was hard to decipher, but time would bring him into her space, when oceans cried out in a spate. Since mother died, Nirmala waited in the evenings with a red lantern, regardless of the moon or a moonless night, near the Long River and sang a psalm for Sirius to scintillate a way for Siddhartha, new lines to light up his palms.

Nirmala named her son Prasada. She lamented and waited for the arrival of a specific boat. Prasada was now much older. She lamented because Siddhartha, whom she didn't believe to be dead, still had not come for her, way past her plumy years. Her mother had passed with time, and she was lain to rest in the river bed, Nirmala in tow, now in her shoes was next, her place in time, her own aged hands, age marks, the deep furrows, burrowed away on her face. On the edge of the Long River lawn, her desires were still strong; her mad little heart looped out of her depths that Siddhartha would be sailing up any day. But her son didn't believe in his mother's madness. He argued and cajoled her to come away with him to the City of Delights she knew only too well, around the same river bend.

Siddhartha lay in his hammock. One night, under a starry sky, a shooting star whispered to him to make a wish; he wished to bring Nirmala back into his life. Without her, this life was bleak. He went into a deep sleep. He was rowing a boat to and fro, along a fertile river bank, taking it in its stride, oaring its vastness. A gold moon took a shine to him, he peered at every port. It was a long river, so many hamlets and hurdles to cross that it was nearly impossible, whose young face he held in the centre of his heart. The throbs egged him on to seek her out. Only she could put out this feverish fire which bore a hole through his body and his soul.

The stars and the moon had not flirted with him, they told him the truth that it wasn't a whim, that he must steer his boat along the Long River bend. She beckoned him night in and night out with a red lantern whose lights could not be put out. She must have her last dance on the timeline steep incline. They murmured to him, "Follow our instructions. Go to The Garden of Love and Delight, and take it from there, before it is too late. Time is elusive, too powerful even for us, though we are the celeste and the heavenly bodies themselves; in time, we also burn up. Unlike us, whom everyone can see such as the stars and the moon, no one can see time, only intuit; truly, time is abstract."

Siddhartha woke up with a jolt and felt a chill run straight through. It felt surreal that he should follow this dream, a dream where he saw Nirmala beckoning him to come to her, before it was too late, before time axed her here, and annexed her, elsewhere. He thought of the distance he would have to cover. A seafarer, he was adept in traversing the seas, he must reach out to her. He was mapping a nautical gauge. He engaged a telescope to see the guiding lights. His ship's handy compass was his destiny. But a storm was also imminent, and he was soon caught up in the midst of it, tackling the high seas, and navigating through a rage-filled welkin was difficult.

The welkin knew about the duo's strength. It dared to cut out destiny; it braved adversities, and storms, as they danced with time, the enigmatic existential gasses, and aurora borealis, whose power dances churned out events, made life possible on earth, then disappeared in a whiff of smoke out of a magic box. Siddhartha could not have

39

smoked this one out. Today, he fought the storms, a shipwreck had occurred, wrenched it apart, pushed its body parts down. Heaving waves blanketed the ocean's rippled surface. Magnificent lightening cracked up the welkin.

He resurfaced, swam, and tried to clamber to a higher ground. For three days, he swam around poisonous tentacles, the jellyfish tantalisingly close. He saw pink sunrises and orange sunsets, buoyed by the waves on his back. Nirmala's memory kept him going: her face, her dance, her body smell loading up his senses, until he closed his eyes, and lost consciousness, falling through a rip in the oceanic blanket. By the red lantern, Nirmala sat alone, the mother of his child, as her mother saw it coming, river in a spate was when he would come for her, and Nirmala believed it. She felt a surge in her heart; she called out his name, "Siddhartha, wake up, wake up, my love, wake up..."

She stood up, and began to dance with the cosmos. She moved the heavens and the earth, she cast a spell on the gods, so they would let her Siddhartha dance, she danced, she twirled like the whirling dervishes, Sufis in a trance. Time was of the essence; a finale was closing in. In the low, sallow lantern, she viewed the Long River, the waves signalled in the moonlight, a sacrifice had to be made. What sort of sacrifice was it, had she not made enough? Her mother, her dance, her youth and beauty. What more? Prasada was all she had left. She couldn't lose him too. What a cruel joke? Have mercy, she cried out to the silent moon; the silver waves gushed grievance. Sentient, they certainly were not.

A fishing boat pulled up Siddhartha onboard, not long after his body went adrift. Sailors tried to resuscitate him; the mute gods heard Nirmala's cries, and saw her spell-binding dance with time. They afforded exceptional munificence. They extended the heavenly fires to him. An enchantress,

Nirmala opened up her soul to the gods; her dancing feet never missed a beat until the gods were in step to her rhythm. Siddhartha was beat, but wasn't going to beat it. He breathed out and in. His dendrites were incandescent. He sat up. The skipper docked his ship at the heartland of the City of Delight, where dancers danced for the nightriders.

He felt better already, for the magic word "dancer" raised an expectation. The term raised a wand in his mind. He tied a band around his forehead determined to find Nirmala. Fortuitously, this time, he believed she wouldn't go too far down the Long River. His blindfold was finally off. As the stars twinkled, he set out with the sailors towards the dancing school. They met many large-eyed, spirited beauties: courtesans in the prime of their youth, luscious and skilful. Siddhartha went quietly around the back into The Garden of Love and Delight and saw a decrepit bed of roses bedding only nettles and thorns; the garden had aged, but aired Nirmala's lily smell, still pervasive, tickling his nostrils.

He cried out, "Nirmala, Nirmala,' it reverberated in the quiet night, an eager owl flew by, a boy was asleep in the darkness. He woke up. It was Prasada.

"Who are you?' Prasada asked.

"I heard you call my mother, Nirmala, were you really calling her name out loud or was I dreaming? I'm her son, Prasada."

"Nirmala has a son? Are you my Nirmala's son?" Siddhartha asked.

"Yes, I'm her's. Who are you?" Prasada asked.

"Take me to her," Siddhartha said.

Prasada had come here to learn about the arts, from this academy of dance, his mother's alma mater.

On the bend of the meandering Long River, Prasada led

the way. Nirmala saw a glow over the horizon. She heard a song she knew too well: time to pack up the boat, my lord, for I'm tired, couldn't row anymore. She stood up and peered into the river. The glow was coming from a lantern on the deck of a boat. It came up close, the singing faded, the boat stopped at the edge of the Long River, two figures jumped out, a silver-haired man with her own, Prasada.

"Who…? Who is it…?"

Siddhartha came up to her, and took her hand to raise the red lantern. It slipped and fell from his hand in this ebony night. He brought it closer to her face. All the clocks in the world couldn't time this somnolent moment, how long they stood lost into each other. This moment had no pasts, no presents, no futures. Both of their eyes welled up, no regrets, no sorrows, but in joyful tears.

He was home, she was his; the boy was theirs; the night cloaked them well. He took her in his arms, she lay her head on his distending chest. They danced as did the dog star in The Garden of Love and Delight, along with the waves, the tireless cosmos. The steps measured perfectly, one, two and a three, through to infinity, which time could not have wrinkled, nor break its circle of mathematics.

"You look like the first day," Siddhartha whispered.

"You look like the first day," Nirmala smiled.

First published by Otoliths, *The Southern Autumn*: Issue 69, Australia, April 2023

Of the Blue Evening

The Queen of the Corvidae went into labour. On this blue evening, her daughter stepped into the kingdom with her foot first. The king named her Dusky, alluding to the time of her birth, the short transition between the night and day. Just as well, the timing was as significant as the name held a magical ring to it. Dusky had no control over when she was born. But the King had a choice over the name. What's in a name? The fact of the matter was, the fledgling had a strange premonition on a blue evening.

Princess Dusky looked the part too; regal. She wore a full moon bindi on her forehead like a jewelled crown of the night. The moon deity Selene anointed her with a prophecy of this glossy spell. A third eye shone the brightest in the aura of this charmed hour. Dusky soliloquised the origin and the force of her bindi to the wild grass and thorny wattle hedges from a high branch of a banyan tree.

One morning her father lay in state; the Corvids swore her in as the new Queen. Large Feather Rook stood by her as minister. The Queen chose the blue evenings to be the most auspicious hours to hold all of her courts. In the interest of her kingdom and its subjects, she and her courtiers planned a significant expansion. Dark days were pickling. An infestation of crows scouring the skies was spotted by the lighthouse on the edge of the North Sea. Each crow returned with a little something caught between their beaks; war booty gathered from the ravaged homes they ransacked. They dropped them off before Queen Dusky and Minister Rook – mango pickles, straw, wheat grains, whatever they found, her majesty's loyal crows brought them all to her beak. In the waxing moon, Queen Dusky's army of crows garnered strength in its shadow.

Across the North Sea lighthouse, nestled within a mango grove, a hut was situated on the far side of a beach. In the first light of the sun, an odd crow flew into this hut. It squatted on a mat of pickled mangoes spread out in the morning's dust. The crow looked around and saw a woman sitting nearby ogling it; the audacious crow ogled back at her while it protruded its feathery neck to peck her pickles. In the open yard, she kept an eye on her prized possession; the mangoes she had been drying and pickling for over a month now. She frowned at the rasping creature. Aghast, she stood up and took a broom she'd placed against a matted wall. After sweeping the front yard meticulously and rolling out a mat, she'd spread the pickled mangoes on it. Despite mangoes being in season, a summer of discontent was unfolding.

"You dirty crow, get off! Get off my pickles! Do you think you can fly in with your dirty feet and trample all over them? Get off – get off my pickles!"

The crow moved only an inch as it continued to peck and prod. Her annoyance grew and she shooed it off with the broom like a magic wand crying, "go – go – get away – get away, you shameless, spineless creature." After a few rough lashes on the crow's back, it flew away, cawing. A neighbour was passing and heard her scream. She stopped at the entrance, and saw how the crow was driving her to madness. Brazen as it was, the crow swooped and sat on the branch of a mango tree overlooking her hut. Some of the tree's longer twigs fell heavily on the shack's fence, where she plucked her mangoes. Unfettered, the crow skipped over closer to her neighbour's fence.

The neighbour had her threshing out in the sun. Without blinking, the crow apprehended her wheat. Unfair it sure was from the pickle woman's perspective, however, the crow also had a point. It felt it had every right to be here, as much as those two women did. "Whose land do they think this was? Was it theirs?" The crow thought. Regardless of whose land it was, it decided to finish what it had come for. To rob whatever it could, and then make a clean egress. It had been scheming, and raiding in waves to take more until its little nest was so crammed with people's granaries that it needed a bigger nest, in spite of its fledglings having left home.

Unlike the hut-dwellers, the crow hadn't purchased its nest through a monetary transaction, signed paper or stamped contracts. It also hadn't acquired the taste of ownership, unlike those two women. It knew that it may have to fly away at any time if there was a storm, or if some wanton earthling wrecked the nest with slingshots. Who knows? Anything was possible on this blue planet.

"Unbeknownst to them," it thought. "Something much larger was brewing in Queen Dusky's court with the advent of the first phase of the moon. Her soldiers were reckless. They could push out those two women and others like them from the neighbourhood as sure as this fair day. These were trying times. Caw, caw, caw. They couldn't even fly. Where would they go if they lost everything and became homeless?"

The pickle woman looked over her shoulder and wondered what the wretched crow was talking about. She picked up her broom again and hurled it over the fence to stop it from cawing. The neighbour who was watching said. "Monowara Begum, you're picking a fight with a crow? Why not cover the pickles with a sieve or something? When you leave them exposed, it's an open invitation to them. It's in their nature. Of course they would drop by and leave their droppings all over the pickle mat."

"Yeah, yeah. Have you covered your threshing?"

"No, I don't have a sieve large enough to cover all my wheat."

"Exactly. That bloody crow is creating mayhem at your

place, leaving its droppings on your grains as you said, and you know what? You don't even know where it has been. Check your wheat now, Ayesha. Crows are there already and they couldn't care less."

This alerted Ayesha. She brisked up her pace sloppily down the path towards her own hut. Monowara Begum sat at her pickle mat and scanned it for any possible droppings. She found a few clusters of faeces in one corner, and some in the middle. Grumbling, she took them out with a torn piece of newspaper and tossed it over the fence. "What's with the crows? Do they think they own all this, that they can simply fly in and out as they wish? Rubbish."

She thought of the newspaper as a possible cover, but the sunlight wouldn't even penetrate it. While she was deciding and looking for a sieve, the crowd of crows on her mat increased. She quickly ran outside to pick up her broom from under the mango tree. When she came back, she spotted more faeces on the mat with some heavily pasted pickles like wet dye on grey hair.

"Why?" Monowara Begum cried. "What horrible fate? Do I not have the same fate as my mother? She had become a homeless refugee because of the atrocities of the redtails. Now this—" The crows cawed and excreted even more. They saw how she was cleaning up after them, and laughed at her. Monowara looked positively miserable while they had their little glow party on the mat. What was she going to do now, the crows conferred?

"As long as crows rule, she needn't do anything else. All we need is access to her food and straw," Elder Jay cawed.

The passerines don't think they own the earth, unlike the redtails. They kill, torture, and steal land in the name of the crown. They call it crown property. But we would never cause such harm, because we are far more discerning. Life is short. Sentiments of ownership, and materialism are meaningless. Our loot is not the Queen's either. Although we may offer her some," Nutcracker cawed.

"Humans mock and trivialise us."

"Not anymore, they won't. They shall see the errors of their ways soon. We shall shed fascinating insights, far better."

"They hunt us for pleasure. Shoot us down because we are a nuisance to them. Our voices are too loud, harsh and brash. How do we get them to understand our worth, our value as scavengers?"

They heard the pickle woman wailing over her spoiled pickles. She would starve tonight and for many nights after. She may have to beg, and only God knows what else she would have to do. The crows had taken everything, including her home. She looked at the thatched roof where the straws had been taken out of place. They poked and beaked the matted walls until the hut was shaken to its core; only a bare mango tree stood outside the fence.

The next morning, Monowara went out in search of food. She saw her neighbour. Her wheat was gone too.

"What should we do?" Monowara asked.

"I don't know. Crows have taken everything we ever had."

"What about your crop fields?" Monowara asked.

"Crows have destroyed those, too," Ayesha responded.

"Really?"

"Yeah," Ayesha said.

"Well, I'm going to see Queen Dusky and Minister Rook. Do you want to come?" Monowara asked.

"No, you go on. I've heard this new Crow Queen isn't any better. Let me know what they say."

At dusk, Monowara set off, rowing a boat across the great North Sea. The Ministry of Crows was housed on top of a knotty banyan tree by an algae-filled pond and crested wheatgrass. Queen Dusky and Minister Rook were perched on two hanger ledges, enthroned at the top of the aerial roots. Monowara thought the Queen looked as if she were in a trance. No matter, what does she know about royalty and her sedated expressions? She only chased crows who fed on her pickles.

Queen Dusky and Minister Rook's hangers were made of sugarcane straw. Monowara recognised them. These were the very straws which the crows had removed from her hut. Monowara approached them, armed with her complaint. She bowed. Flapping her large wings, Queen Dusky made a gesture for her to speak.

"An army of crooked crows have attacked us and have taken everything my neighbour and I had," she said.

"What have they taken? Pickles? Wheat?" Minister Rook asked in Monowara's language.

"Yes, pickles, wheat, and more," she said.

"What do you mean?" Minister Rook asked.

"They picked out sugarcane straws from my roof and poked holes in it. I've got no roof over my head."

"My crows did that and left you two out of joint?"

Minister Rook and Queen Dusky laughed.

"Yes, they did. They left us bare. Do you not believe me?"

Monowara looked around and pointed at their perching hangers, and all the nibble-sized pickles all over the wheatgrass at the crowfoot's nimble play.

"Look, look, my pickles which your army took. I eat them for dinner every day, and sell pickled mangoes. Do you not see them right here?" she asked. "Your thrones are also made of sugarcane straw which had kept my roof together until they were beaked out."

"Where is your proof, woman?" Rook asked. "These are royal thrones. Are you accusing us of robbery?"

"What more proof do you need? These are mine, my signature pickles, and my straws. I have a signed and stamped contract from the state which says the land and the hut belong to me."

"Let me ask, when you say it is yours – your pickle, your land and hut, and straws. Do you see your name written anywhere in all these?"

"No, of course not. The contract does. It's from the high court."

"Ah! The high court of the redtails, not from the court of Goddess Selene?" Queen Dusky asked.

"Goddess Selene? What do you mean?"

"Surely, land belongs only to Her. Pickles too, no rains – no pickles, right? What rights do you have to make any claim?"

The crow courtiers cawed in unison. The Queen continued. "Since the deity hasn't put your name down on anything, do you really own what you tout? Her land was bequeathed to us because She willed it. If She wants, She can take it back, and us too, anytime," Queen Dusky's voice, becoming husky.

"Crows can't do this. Did the deity give them the right to fly in and out of our land as they please and grab whatever they please? Why, this is utter madness!"

"The land is no more yours than it is the crows. They have misappropriated nothing from you. You, on the other hand, have claimed Her land, Her dirt, Her rocks as yours. It was the crow's ploy to put you out of misery. It is you who have stolen, robbed, and kept it as yours. Confess."

"Rubbish! Crows have looted. It's criminal. If any, they have put us into misery more than you know. Are you any different from the redtails?" Monowara snapped. This was exhausting.

"Moving forward, our rule of law is not to own private property. Land belongs to the Almighty Selene. We don't

49

do bodily harm. Nothing is carried out in my name, either. Unlike the greedy redtails, victors such as us do not 'steal', 'tout' or 'loot' – a fair bit of difference, no? My crows aren't the bandit villains you take them to be."

"You also steal," Monowara argued.

"The sun also rises," Queen taunted.

"Meaning?" Monowara asked.

"You'll see. Join us, become a crow. You'll find it liberating," Queen said.

"I'm not a crow," Monowara said.

Monowara inclined her head and spotted a flock of crows coming towards her. She left the court. She retraced her steps and sat down by the algae-filled pond outside the banyan hedge. The crows followed her there and performed circles of a flying ritual around her head. "What did they say? Was my name written on the rocks? They are trying to put you out of misery. Become a crow."

The world was Selene's to give away. But the redtails had a different view – possession of the land and draconian rules. The Queen's insightful, lofty words were lost on Monowara. Kaleidoscopic patterns of layered realities were reflected in the pond. It mirrored an endgame. The Corvids weaponised their vision to free Monowara from the redtails. In the rising sun a new order was born; a utopian Crowland spearheaded by a buck-naked Queen of Crows. In the mango grove, crows rebuilt Monowara's hut again. It was on a debt free, no man's land where an aged Monowara crowed with delight while she chewed her pickles; her scavengers' impatience grew, nature of the beast.

However, the heavenly bodies also moved. In the interplay, the moon was in the earth's shadow as it progressed into its last phase. Queen Dusky's bindi darkened into a total eclipse. Boasting her vast feathery cape, she trotted down to a corner of her large hanger. Within the short span of the dusk, Dusky flew away with a murder of crows into the depths of the blue evening. Only a glib westerly wind blew over the bleak, and timeless rocks of a borrowed land.

_____

First published by *The Gorko Gazette*, USA, August 2023

The Giver

Morning

Last summer, when the days were waning, my young neighbour Poultu, a twelve-year-old, entered through my garden gate, sweating profusely. He stumbled over a loose plank on the garden path.

"What's wrong?" I asked.

"The panipuri man has returned. Kids are going missing again."

"Don't worry."

"What? Why not?"

"I'll make sure to protect you."

Poultu ran back up the path, and I sat down in a cane chair out on the veranda with a cup of white tea which my maid made, and brought it out. I also heard the man crying futchka/panipuri as he headed down the alley. This irresistible street snack, much like ice cream is an absolute darling of a snack both for adults and children. I thought of what Poultu was saying earlier about a connection between children being snatched and this panipuri man, yet another remake of Steven King's horror nightmares. I hoped not.

I finished tea. I rose and walked through the hallway. My grandmother's silver three-level pandan, or where she buried all her betel leaves and nuts, sat on a corner table right up to the wall. I unlidded it and took out a slivered nut and popped it into my mouth. Putting the cover back, I flip-flopped along the long hallway, dragging my chappals all the way to the end of it, and into my grandmother's room. She was sitting in a reclining chair by the window looking pensive out into the void. When she saw me standing at the door, she asked me to sit down on her bed, opposite her.

Gramma was an open book. I could read her anytime. I looked at her and I knew straight away that she wished to give, again. Why was she so generous? I often asked myself. What satisfaction did she get from it all? She did all her charities through me, too. Today, she told me that she wished to give Poultu's family some money. I wondered why? Why his family? Why not the others, who might have lost something really huge such as children to the grabber, whoever he maybe, the panipuri man that Poultu suspected, who knows? But Gramma never told me the real deal about her charities. She asked me to get her pandan, sending me back to the hallway.

I brought her the pandan. She uncovered the antique container and pulled out a paan leaf from its deep bottom. She made a triangular paan for herself with a sprinkling of slivered betel nut and a swipe of lime. She mouthed it and tucked it in one of her cheeks, which balled out. She looked at me and smiled.

"I want you to withdraw fifty thousand takas from the bank tomorrow and take it to Poultu's family."

"Why? Gram, why Poultu of all the people on earth? I asked.

"I'll tell you a story tonight. Come back at midnight when the world sleeps," she said.

"Does the world really ever sleep?" I asked with a flicker of laughter in my eye.

"Whether the world actually slept or not, is not the question. The question you should be asking is, "What really happens when we believe the world is asleep?"

"What happens? I asked.

"As I said, I'd tell you at midnight."

53

She was clearly evasive. But it piqued my curiosity. I wanted to know what she was going to tell me. Maybe, she could clue me into the grabber who had been taking all the children; undeniably these children went missing every time the panipuri man emerges in the alley. I couldn't wait for midnight to come that day. But the sunny afternoon, for now, made me restive. I went out. I took her pandan back to its place in the hallway and strolled out of the garden path through which Poultu had entered a couple of hours ago.

Afternoon

The panipuri man stood with his paraphernalia on a cart at a specific spot down the alley, a few steps away from our house. In measured steps, I approached the man. He looked at me and I thought his pupils darted a few times. I asked him to plate me a regular. With a dash of everything, he rushed to make a plate of six large panipuri and handed it over. I felt trepidation from his eye movement. Did he know that he was a prime suspect? After all, children did get kidnapped every time he was around. Then, I saw Poultu playing cricket with the alley boys.

I felt something for the children, then. I looked the panipuri man straight in the eye. His left thumb trembled. He began to stir the chickpeas really fast on his makeshift kerosene stove.

"What's going on?" I finally asked.

"What? What do you mean?" he asked.

"What I mean is this: why do children go missing every time you come by?"

"Ask your grandmother," he said.

"Gramma? How do you know her? Have you sold panipuri to her, too?"

"Ask her?"

Walling me out, he turned around on his heels with his

back towards me. I could only see his checked shirt, of black and white large squares, and the back of his black curly hair. Fair enough, I told myself. Tonight, the mystery will be solved. I left the man and his panipuri cart behind me and sauntered towards the bank. I joined the long queue of clients.

Midnight

Calm had descended. The unpaid piper had piped in the Hamelin children of the alley indoors; they slept at midnight. As a hand full of bindi stars surfaced on the smooth sky, I headed towards Gramma's room in my sleepers and my chappals. Gramma had a hurricane burning in the corner of the room. She sat on the same chair as before, and I sat on the same spot of her bed. I looked at her paper, wrinkled face; time had aged her. With an awful lot of questions, a wick was also burning inside of me like the wick of the glassed hurricane lamp.

"Land. They grabbed lots, and tucked it away nearly at every corner, like an obsessive disorder. Worms were warming up under. Worms are good for the soil. One day, they hired a young boy as a caretaker, whose job was to sweep away dead, fallen leaves and bird pooh to make compost. However, these were empty land, without anyone ever visiting or anything ever being grown or built on them. The young boy started weeding and seeding, turning it in and out until the soil was ready. By now, the boy was much older, his bones stretched and shaped gnawing through growing pains. His young limbs and child look disappearing, gradually being transformed, as though the child he once was never existed. Snitched. No matter. The land too had transformed into a productive patch of vegetables and fruits. The barren, infertile land was gone. That boy had a green thumb, you see."

Gramma coughed and sighed. I sat listening with bated breath.

"One day, it happened."

"What? What happened?" I asked.

"As the boy was pruning a dormant guava tree, he found a bone."

She stopped. She swallowed hard. Perspiration springing up her wrinkles.

"What? Are you sure?" I asked.

I moved edgily on the edge of the bed.

"Although, the boy was much older, but had not still fully fledged. He found not one, but many as he kept on digging. He dug tirelessly. All of the lands were full of them. Those small bones, the much-loved bones. The boy had no idea who was behind all this. A child's find, frightening as it was, one day he came to me and told me. The place was also my favourite walking trail. I told him to quit. And the next day gave him some start-up money. He took it and bought a panipuri cart."

It still didn't add up. Who are "they"? Why did the children disappear only when this boy was in the alley? Why was this never mentioned to the police? Why did Gramma pay such a huge amount of money to Poultu's family and not to the others? If she was the giver, she should give equally, in all fairness. What plot was she weaving, what cosmic rip was she suturing?

"The boy grew up into a panipuri young man, eventually shedding his young limbs. He then ran away in fear after he had discovered all the dead bones. When the police found out, they interrogated him. Instead of going after the grabber of bones, they wanted to pin him down. They even put him in jail, I bailed him out. One of the officers was Poultu's father. I paid him, and I continue to pay him to keep the files closed for the sake of the boy."

56

I ran my five fingers through my hair. Still, the loose ends bothered me. Why can't the panipuri man sell elsewhere? Why does this selling have to be in the same alley where the grabber was still active? And how did Gramma know that he wasn't the snatcher? Did she know them?

"To prove his innocence, his presence must be felt in the same alley where Poultu's father, the officer could see him in clear daylight, not running away. Sure, the kidnapping always happened around him. But the snatcher hid in plain sight. Since the bones were found, the land had been cleared and vacated. But the mystery remained. Where was the grabber burying the bones, and why was he more active around the panipuri seller? The police hadn't cracked any of those mysteries, yet. However, my nagging suspicion is perhaps the snatcher is using the boy as the fall guy or a decoy, knowing that without further evidence the police could not incriminate him. While the grabber of bones, continued to haunt and chew, the panipuri man bore the brunt of policing until proven guilty. Besides, I'm paying them too, to keep him out of jail."

I jolted. I saw Gramma's face turn ghastly white in the hurricane light. Her death stares moved my glance away to picture the young beauty she once was in her prime. As I made my way out, she stood in my way.

"Who owns this land, do you know?" I asked plainly.

"The Giver?"

_____

First published by *Kitaab*, Singapore, 2023

Aina Ghar/The Mirror Room

Between a three-hundred-year-old house of the Sufis, and an un-gated front yard, a quiet graveyard sleeps, where the bones of the ancestors rest. The spiritual leadership of this complex changes hands every time the previous Sufi dies, and a new one is designated to the cushion called the *Gaddi*. who is then called the *Gaddi Nashin Pir* belonging to a seven-hundred years old Sufi dynasty tradition. His office is situated in the *Aina Ghar* or the mirror room. Why is the office room called the Aina Ghar? It does not resonate the Versailles' great hall of mirrors, at all.

Still, this Aina Ghar keeps all the records through those seven-hundred years of history piled up on its dusty, cobweb-filled crusty shelves, and books about the Gaddi Nashins which even the many restorations cannot erode. History, for better or for worse, is cast in stone, never eroded, just unchangeable, unmitigated stories of the past. History. Unlike kings or nawabs, the Sufis are spiritual leaders, who guide people through the darkest hours of despair, grief, unaccomplished tasks and unfulfilled dreams in the Aina Ghar, where people sit on the clay floor and confide to the Sufi within its four walls, who does not judge, only listens and then provides a solution. People, return happy after every counsel.

One day a boy comes to the Sufi, looking for a friend. The Sufi replies that his friend lies in that grave below, under there, not in the higher grounds here, simply by pointing his index finger towards the family graveyard in the front. The walking distance is not much. Just outside the arched gate. The boy leaves him. As he comes out of the Aina Ghar and waits near the grave's gate, he remembers a dream from last night, in which the friend appears here, in the Aina Ghar itself. *The boy asks, "Why* are you here?" The friend replies, "These days, this is where I live, these days."

The dream enlightens him about his friend. He learns about his demise this morning from the Sufi in the mirror room. *In the dream, the friend has a clown mask on. His face is painted white; his lips are red and widely stretched, grinning. The boy begins to wail calling his friend's name out loud, "Usmaan, Usmaan where are you?" in a crowded bazaar. So many people, so many souls, but not one says, he is Usmaan.*

That's how the dream transpires in juxtaposed fragmented realities – first a man, who says he lives here nowadays, then a grinning clown; the boy's search for Usmaan in a crowded bazaar. The Sufi shows him the way where to find his bones, for his body has pulverised by now deep under six feet of heavy weeds and nettles, pushing up the daisies. Growing up in these alleys not far from the Aina Ghar which stands solid as a rock through fluid time which slips and slops like a river to what end, eludes the Sufi. When a body is transported, this short span from the house to the tomb after its life ends, the Sufi prays and commemorates the dead soul without a drop of tear.

Yet, the Aina Ghar continues as a repository of knowledge of all the dead peoples' tales when they were alive. Here to there, that's how short the long journey is. In the seven-hundred years of the Sufi dynasty, there's where the bones of the forefathers rest; a young, restless Sufi rises to the Gaddi, as a Gaddi Nashin Pir.

———————

First published by *RIC Journal*, Bangalore/Paris, May 2023

Oneness

"For a moment there, I became you and you me, my love. I expressed the words you wished to hear all your life, and you whispered what I believed to be the holy grail," Rowena texted.

"Then why can't we do what we are meant to do?" Abrar texted back.

"We can't because we are not in the one bubble. In the spirit we are. You were kindred in that moment, but in that moment, only," she wrote.

"What happens in that moment?" he asked.

"In that moment, we clashed into each other and found ourselves in oneness; we metamorphosed into one ball of emotions. We ceased to be individuals," she wrote.

"What's wrong with that?" he wrote back.

"Everything. When we stop being what we are. We become non-entities. We lose our sense of judgement, our sense of morality and identity."

"Isn't that what we are in that moment, this craving to be one? The desire to defuse and fuse to find a new entity as one into a single bubble of passion instead of being two identities, instead of being two ships passing – two bubbles floating abreast?"

"That's exactly who we are. Two ships passing closely enough for a touch perhaps, but never to become a whole."

"What's the point of living then?" he asked.

"The whole point of living is to be in a paradox – we live only because we die. All marching in a procession where our ancestors had been at the forefront of that march once. Who goes first and who goes last is determined by time and time alone. Albeit, we must all be in that destined journey of life and death."

"In the bubble of oneness, one of us can extricate from this procession, no? As we go together whenever our time is prime."

"Ah but can we?" she asked.

"Why not?"

" 'Cause, my love, time will cut a wedge between us even within that bubble of oneness we shall lose, and time and time again, time shall win, as though there were no tomorrows, no yesterdays and no todays. In this oneness, we couldn't reach out to the stars together. Perhaps, in time, we shall become infinite like time itself. In its capacity to hold us and see us through to eternity. Even eternal love, who knows, but not as you wish, my love."

"Yet, I want to be in that bubble: the bubble of oneness. So be it, until time removes one of us, capricious it may be because who could tell who would drop out of this precession first. Who could tell? I could still love you, even if I lost you; it would still be worth it.

"Maybe, until my clothes size becomes smaller and smaller. I start to wear my children's clothes, while they wear mine in reversed order like Benjamin Button. Until I dissolve in those clothes and disappear. 'Cause that's when I drop out of the procession, and from the bubble of oneness too. Can you live without me then, without love, as an insider of the bubble of love?"

"That was the moot wasn't it? I whispered to you, to be in separate bubbles," he wrote.

"I voiced your wish to be inside that bubble with you," she texted.

"Why aren't we then, my love?" he asked.

Silence fell after that: a moment of pure enchantment in the bubble of love.

First published by *Micro Fiction*, Quail Bell, USA, January 2023

61

River of Melted Chocolate

A full house at the movies did not deter people from pouring into the theatre hall. They came in droves from every walk of life to watch a much anticipated movie, called *Chocolate River*. The wealthy sat separately in VIP lounges for paying more and the poor took all the front seats and in the passageways when there were no more seats available. *Chocolate River*, a horror movie, wasn't just the regular gore and blood bath of a Viking wasteland of bones and skeleton-filled war-field. But was produced by a producer who had a penchant for movies with a spiritual bent. The characters were almost ethereal, who flaunted a sprite like existence in abstraction so skilfully contrived that viewers only saw these characters mediated through marked footsteps on chocolate, melting into a river.

The viewers paid good money to watch this movie which was cutting edge, abstracting the spirit from the body, a performance which could be sensed through the delineation of a physical environment viewers were acutely aware; it depicted a physical house, blue with a red pointy roof, where people presumably gathered to have a party. Guests were arriving in all sorts of vehicles such as horse-driven carriages, fiery chariots, buses even, electric cars, bicycles, and scooters, scooting to this house. However, when the vehicles stood in front of the house the viewers didn't see anyone egressing, or stepping out apart from these vehicles parked as a sign of this gathering. Surely, those vehicles were driven by human hands and feet carrying passengers who should be all getting off or getting out at some point, now that they had been parked in front of the house for a while?

Inside the theatre hall people were eager to watch human bodies. They got increasingly restive, fidgeting sloppily to the front edge of their small seats. Those who had the cheapest seats tried to inch away from being crammed between people so close that they could smell the body odour tickling their nostrils. As much as they wanted, they could not inch farther away sideways or forward, without colliding into those sitting next to them. The only way out was to keep shifting from corner to corner, backward and forward in the cramped seats. With very little room to manoeuvre, some elbowed each other on a common armrest, causing rash, brash tiffs. For those who sat in luxurious VIP lounges, their distress was noted differently; they stood slinking up and down the space, frowning, gazing at the white silver screen, sighing, then finally sinking down in the leather upholstered soft cushions, drinking red wine served on the house. Occasionally, holding hands of kin sitting next to them; no wine or bread for the cheap seats up in the front.

A quarter of an hour had lapsed, and still, no sign of a human body was visible on the silver screen. The doors of the big house opened and closed. Opened again and closed again with a bang as though turbulent winds had been appointed as watch guards to usher in the new arrivals. The house was soundproof. The outsiders, the viewers in the theatre hall heard nothing, only imagined what the insiders did or possibly were doing. Even the walls didn't seem to have any ears. All ears into the movie, but they heard nothing, let alone saw what the guests were doing. Were they laughing, perhaps? Drinking or maybe breaking into mayhem within those rooms of the blue house and pointy red roof, misbehaving, a full-on brawl. Dancing with the idiosyncratic Mad Hatter, romancing, supping with kings and queens, or sipping tea with scones and clotted cream.

It was hard to decipher. The movie was as colourless as a whiteboard and characterless as chalk in its depiction of abstraction. Their vehicles, however, sparkled which stood in defiance of this rare and odd masquerade; by contrast, which were gold-plated carriages, electric cars, and rubber wheels that the makers could lick. Speaking of which, gold the densest metal of all, copper and rubber, these carriers journeyed, yet a thousand miles, a fair bit to get here. Without any annoyance, through spacetime to this resting place tonight where the party was being held. Now those vehicles were parked before this pointy house as the winds took the guests inside, one step forward, two steps backward, one step in, two steps out, swaying sideways in the breeze.

How long the party was going to last was unknown. The viewers were clueless and grotty. They felt they needed a break from watching this absurd story with no beginning or end. Ah but, the beginning, a starting point was impossible to figure out; infinity derived from non-ending circles. Still, there had to be a starting point where the movie was emergent. At which point, though? Did it even have a starting point? The viewers began to ruminate and doubt its integrity which held much promise, that they came in droves to watch this bold movie. Now, the novelty was thinning. The spectators felt like a hostage to such a plotless, pointless movie without a proper premise.

Were they missing something? In the VIP lounge, the VIPs grumbled over how it was such a waste of their time and money to buy these expensive tickets. They even began to make plans for a full refund. Instead of watching the movie they held a meeting to make the owner of the theatre hall accountable; to ask for a refund. If he refused, they would take legal action, sue the owner, drag him through the courts if necessary for subjecting them to this insanity. There was a unanimous decry against the movie and the movie owner both in the upper and the lower halls.

It sure was courageous; however, just then the doors of

the theatre hall also opened. A ticket man stood at the door beckoning the watchers. At first, no one understood. Then he began to swing an axe as vigorously as he could to signal that he was "telling" them to leave not "asking". The VIPs were told to exit first. They stood up and appeared on the door's threshold. They blinked at what they saw. No less, but the most incredible house from the movie. It stood before them, right here and now – the big blue house with a red pointy roof floating over the melting chocolate river, its doors shutting and opening; the golden carriages were still parked, so were all the chariots, the bicycles, and the scooters, the busses, and the electric copper-wired cars.

The ticket man told them to enter the house. They did, followed by those, too, from the cheap seats all the way to the end of the hall's long passageways. What became of them was all over on the silver screen. However, there were none to watch; the theatre hall had emptied.

First published in *Popshot Quarterly Special Collector's Edition*, Issue 41, Magic, UK, Autumn 2023

Number Ninety-Four

Part I

Her pale face radiant under an August setting sun, she sits on a bench at bus stop 94. There is a rusty covering above. The bench below has pastel green paint peeling off – hard, grim, dour. Waiting for bus no 94; it is late. Instead of searching for an alternative route, she walks a quarter of a mile and waits. Day in and day out. Year in and year out, until one day she turns ninety-four herself.

Her tired eyes stare into oblivion, and notice a solitary, restless daisy through a lonely crack in the cemented road. It is across the bus stop, bobbing its breezy yellow head, anxious, to fly away, had it not been for its root spiralling down through the gaping, jagged cranny. She lets out a sigh; her eyes light up. All she is left with is desires nestled within the cosy warmth of her heart – a place gone cold from the wait.

Where is he? The man? Her one true love? He asks her to pick him up from this very bus stop – the last bus at 94. She wears a pink, floral sari which wraps around her young, smooth body. The bus never comes. She waits hours until the day is gone, afternoon and evening. Still, no sign of buses here. An empty, abandoned stop.

She continues to look at the empty road ahead, in case the bus arrives. The daisies are in full bloom of spring. She hears someone call her name. "Ayesha, Ayesha." Then, "Look, look, I'm here." She turns her head, and a shiver runs through her. She views a bare tree by the river, leaves growing out of it, disproportionately, insanely psychedelic. "Where are you, I don't see you, I don't see you anywhere, Mohabbat, Mohabbat. Where are you, my love? Do you see me?" Ayesha asks. Her heart is swelling. With shallow breaths of excitement, she inhales his faint hair oil

66

dispersed in the air. Anytime, anytime he will be here and pick her up and hold her against his chest. His soft lips pressing down on her lips – ruby red; melding into rich hot chocolate cake.

Part II

At Fajr, Mohabbat Ali Khan wakes up to the sound of the azaan. It drifts through the minaret of a local mosque of his neighbourhood. He descends the narrow stairs and steps outside into a mosaic courtyard and through a floral, inlaid, arched architrave. This mosaic square is fenced in on two sides by stucco brick walls. He nearly sleepwalks towards a tap near the western wall and turns it on to do ablution, wazu, before the namaaz. He begins to wash his hands, elbows, face and ankles three times. Rinses his mouth three times, and three splashes into the nostrils – three splashes for each of the body extremities.

During the partition at the time of independence from the British, his parents opted to stay in India. After they passed, he continued to reside in the old capital of Delhi – in the same house too, the ancestral property. A blue arched house, beautifully antique. Accustomed to communal riots, love-hate relationships are common with Hindus and Christians, as well as with his Parsi friends. He grew up through political turmoil and difficult social and cultural system.

From the other side of these thick walls, he hears the water trickle, as the neighbours, the Dilliwallas, are waking up. Hot tea brews in a shack restaurant. The deep-frying smells of samosas, daal puri, parathas and omelette swim through the morning air. After prayer, Mohabbat Ali Khan steps outside the gates to go for his customary morning walks. Munshi Giasuddin, the local barber's salon down the alley is open early, but he already has a client. He is sitting

67

in a wooden, straight-backed chair by the roadside. Munshi is rubbing up soap on his beard and chatting away. He nods at Mohabbat as he walks past.

Mohabbat walks a mile. His usual rounds are all the way up to the Jama Mosque, and then looping back. He usually performs Fajr at the mosque which takes care of both the namaaz as well as the morning walk. Today, however, he is pressed for time, and prays at home. He looks at the barber through the corners of his eyes and runs a finger absent-mindedly through his thick beard, twisting up his moustache, thinking that his beard also needs a trim. He walks a couple of steps ahead and sits down on a hard bench at the shack restaurant for some hot tea and samosa.

"Salaam Janaab, how are you this morning?" a tea boy asks.

"Walaikummassalam," Mohabbbat replies over a slight cough. "Yeah, I'm very well."

"Tea and samosas? Freshly fried," the tea boy asks.

Mohabbat nods and sees that the tea boy is disappearing around the corner to fetch the order while he sits in the mellow morning light watching the barber's precision cutting next door. His client spits betel saliva occasionally on the side at which the barber lifts his razor sharply away from his face.

Mohabbat has a date today with his Ayesha in an unkempt mossy garden near her house. His eyes dilute just thinking of her. He must wear her favourite hair oil today. His thought is interrupted as his order of tea and hot samosas arrive. He bites into its crunch carefully, sipping and savouring the white tea at the same time. He wants to pop into the barber shop next door after he finishes here.

Over at the barber shop, he looks at all the hair oil bottles from various brands shelved around a glassed window bay. He picks up Jaba Kushum which is her favourite. He pays up at the front and leaves the shop. The barber smiles at him; he leaves with a polite nod.

Mohabbat walks home. He enters through the gate and climbs up the stairs. He decides to take a shower before he leaves for his date. He puts on a white embroidered kurta and pyjamas. He lavishly oils his hair with Jaba Kushum and runs a comb through his beard. He comes downstairs and steps out on the road; he hears howls closing in like the fury of tsunami. He sees a huge mob approaching his house; a sporadic riot is at his gate.

The bus no 94 arrives in time. Mohabbat is lucky to escape the mob's scourge. He stands almost camouflaged against the wall's whiteness. People enter his home, and they drag out his possessions, rattling rusty trunks, his books, his charpai bed, his father's easy chair, hookah, and his violin, hurling them all out on the street in a heap. He says nothing. An innocent bystander, he trudges along the wall with caution until he arrives at the bus stop. He falls a few times before he is able to ascend the bus. He has a sweaty forehead – a few drops fall over his eyelids – and an already wet beard. He wonders if there's a riot also at Ayesha's place. He finds a window seat through the crowd. Stumbling, he sits down.

The bus is moving. He lets out a sigh of relief. Thankfully, there's hope. He is thinking fast to start a new life with Ayesha some place safer, perhaps abroad where there's peace and stability. As long as the bus is moving, there is some hope. He looks around him and sees panic in the wet frowns of his fellow passengers. This bus will take them away where all can rest in peace. Suddenly, an explosion catapults the bus.

69

Part III

Young Ayesha's sweet pink sari comes undone; it is noosed around her neck, strangulated. The pink hue reflects a bluish blush on her silken, smooth skin. This place is eerily deserted. Doctors know better. She lies in a white starched hospital bed. Her skin is decrepit, mottling. Mohabbat is here, coming towards her. She waits; she hears his voice echoing through her comatose brain. She desires to go on a safari with him, maybe not on the unlucky 94 after all. He is smiling… she sniffs the odour… her favourite oil brushed into the strands of his hair. Glib winds whisper into her ears. Ninety-four years of wait cannot atone for this wrong. The bus has changed course. It does not come here anymore.

First published by Decolonial Passage, USA, 2023

Gambit

Julian's eyes sparkled. He looked over his shoulder and found a lonesome deer in the bottom of a stream. It was lapping up water, thirsty from its long walk. Julian took out his camera adjusted the lenses to 300 mm to take a long shot to capture the best angles. He took a few snaps as the deer continued to lap up. Then there was a sudden gun shot. Julian's lenses found people aiming at the deer but missing it. Poachers? Julian grimaced. The deer took off. The poachers followed it as far as they could go. The missed shot would cost them their jobs, perhaps their heads too with the unkind bosses with little tolerance for people without prowess.

The poachers slovenly stopped the midway chase and turned back. Julian had the best shots. A drama was unfurling in the East Wick like the unclasped ferns of this wilderness underway to a new beginning. Julian's powerful lenses followed the poachers all the way to their den – another animal kingdom, unique like every other species of this rainforest. Only, more brutal, they hounded after the blood of their own. More profound hearts could be found in the heart of the forest where the elephants, the giraffes could not bear to kill their own; no one claimed that the forest was easy to negotiate.

A lot happened here. Carcasses lay bare for others to feed. A full on hunger war, bloody face to face battles. But the young poachers now reckoned with their fates. The greedy bosses would not let them be. For the deer had fled, hence, no musk, skin or antlers to trade. The poachers were lined up, one next to the other. Tears and sweats of fear ran down their veins and their bare chests. Powerful men could stir up muck and dust to any level if their hunger was not met; young poachers took the blame, the bane of their lives.

The boys had no escape. They stood like petrified

rabbits before these powerful men, backed by many other powerful men of all sizes and colours. Unless something spectacular happened here today, there was no escape. Heavens had to fall over, tsunamis, to wash away sins, the rain forest had to awaken, the trees had to walk, animals had to talk. Something, anything mythical, extraordinary had to happen to stop this scourge.

It was as if the forest heard the boys' cries. A breathing entity, the forest had a silent but fiery gambit to win this war. The cheetahs, the lions and the jaguars woke up and roared with hunger. They were out to poach for food, too. Their eyes lit up. Julian's eyes steady. His lenses fixed without a tremble. Swelling human smell, coming from a nearby den. The bloodhounds waited for the right moment to pounce. They pounced on whoever was closest to their claws. The poacher boys were in the crosshairs; no one had the gun-men's back; in the forefront to snare.

First published in *Mr Bull Bull Magazine*, USA, 2024

Oasis

After the rain when the sun came out, it shone on the dust-free gardenia leaves. Ruhul just finished praying Zohr on his mat and was folding it away in his stark, rooftop bedroom. The quilt in his bed had not been turned or aired and neither had his pillows been fluffed out since he had woken.

He went into the kitchen and made himself a cup of Darjeeling tea, pouring hot water from a whistling kettle over a dunked, bleached paper tea bag. He picked up the cup and walked to the roof's edge where he could see the garden over the rail. He noticed that a cat had sat all cuddled up on a narrow ledge of a rail on the opposite building's high parapet. He felt insecure for the cat, but the cat sat with its eyes firmly closed on all fours showing no fear and enjoying its freedom on the ledge.

Ruhul was curious that how was it even possible that the cat felt no fear. He could easily transport his trepidations into the cat through the space where he was standing, the way his heart was pounding for it. For once he wished that he was that cat, knew no fear of falling, until a dog next door barked, the cat opened its eyes dully and jumped off the ledge to safety. Ruhul smiled and watched the oasis of the leaves shimmering in his garden between the two tall concrete buildings.

Playing in the dappled lights, the leaves mesmerized him. He forgot to blink. A crow flew across and broke the panacea of the moment. He picked up his cup and took another sip, while a breeze blew a strand of his curly locks over his forehead. Humming a nursery rhyme, he saw a little boy dressed in a white kurta top and pyjamas, and a round white embroidered topi covering his small head, running down a corridor of this house that belonged to his grandparents.

As he ran, he rhymed a nursery song that his grandmother used to sing to him in Urdu – *"nini baba nini makhan roti chini, apne abbu aaye, lal khelona laye, khelte, khelte bhuk lagi, khalo bete momphali, momphali mei dana nei, hum tomahara nana nei, nana gaye Dilli, Dilli se laye billi, billi diya bacche, Allah Mia sacche… nini baba nini…"*

Echoing, the rhyme faded within the sooty, old walls of the narrow, dark corridor. He looked behind him at a girl chasing him; she was more like charging him with a baton. He couldn't see her anymore; she whiffed away in a cloud of smoke as though she didn't even have a bodily existence; this, a figment from the past, he had lived through all those years, the past had dissipated at a swish of a wand. Her name was Usma Tahera. Growing up, Ruhul played with her as a child in the attic of this big house. She was their neighbour's daughter where the cat was lounging.

Mostly, they played dress-as-you-like. Ruhul was King and Usma was his Queen. They would dress as whatever was trunked in the attic, rusty imitation jewellery of de-stoned rings, and clip-on, flashy earrings. Ruhul wore the rings on his fat fingers, and Usma would roll all over the attic floor laughing and calling him a fat King. Ruhul would try to keep his royal cool in his court, while Usma couldn't care less. To her, it was just a fantasy role-play. They even had crowns cut out of cardboard boxes, and decorated with more cut-outs of pasted stars and moons of shiny cellophane wrappers, also tucked away in those dusty trunks.

Magic, it sure was, the past and the present were fused into Ruhul's mind where he stood now on the roof watching the dappled lights in the garden. Nursery rhymes anchored the past into the memory of an underwater sinkhole.

He slurped up the rest of the tea and went indoors. Between now and the Asr prayer, there was some time which

74

he intended to use. Prayers structured his day. He jotted down details of what he was meant to do and when. Even at sunset, at Magrib, he knew what needed to be done. Ramadan was nearing; he needed some groceries. He loved to break his fasts with fried eggplant or onion pakoras or frittatas rolled basun into batter. And piaju badas from daal. This fasting month, the one and only he found most meaningful – Ramadan, replete with spiritual experience came closest to abstraction in which Ruhul found God. Iftar at sunset was the most magical of all moments when he lit a candle out on the roof to break his fast throughout the month.

He scratched his nose and realised he had a red bump. He stopped scratching because it could flare up. Last night, he slept really well. He changed into a pair of black pants and came out of his room. He was going to town. He avoided going downstairs and meeting with the family. He cooked and ate alone in his own rooftop room.

Today was his day off. Normally, he dressed for work. He worked at a cutlery factory in the city near the Madhumita cinema hall. It was called "The Shiny Cuts". The knives were shiny and serrated. But Ruhul laughed out loud every time he thought of the name. The factory owner's son named it, he'd heard once. As though the knives would enhance cutting to a point that the food on the other end would also gleam. But the company was registered under that name and it stuck.

What happened to Usma, though? Even when he felt angry at her for laughing at him, destroying the make-belief world of the kingdom, and breaking all the boundaries of a status quo, he never felt that he would ever do away with her. In his heart, he nurtured a profound tenderness for her and believed that she was the Queen of his heart, where she ruled most seriously. However, it transpired differently in the end game of the real world, where they were just common citizens.

The news of Usma moving abroad fell heavily into the silence of the attic. Her father came downstairs one midday with the news that they were going away. Ruhul's mother invited him to come inside for tea. Ruhul was waiting for Usma as usual in the attic when the bell rang. He peeked through Roman style balustrade and recognized the man. He even overheard the happy babble of good tidings.

He took his crown off without any prattle as though he has had a major blow in a battle. And placed it on the attic floor. She was to go away. Ruhul felt trepidation; his heart missed a beat. It was perhaps love, he wasn't sure but what he decided to do with his young life surely marked a destiny.

Looking back at that dreadful afternoon when it had all come tumbling down for Ruhul, he realised that he had lost both the kingdom as well the love of his life. He couldn't have asked her to stay back for him. They were children; Usma moved to some foreign land.

For several months, he spent time alone in the attic trying to role-play both as King as well the Queen. Gradually, it occurred to him how lonesome he was becoming. As the years rolled on, he outgrew this desire for role-play. He realised, that he needed a saviour. At first, he was unsure as to how he would find one. Over time, it all fell into place. He became a regular at the mosque, praying, fasting, and practicing the whole gamut of spiritualism. Usma was in his waking, in dreaming all around him dancing, laughing like a mountain stream.

Celibacy wasn't something he contemplated on. But it appeared to him that the path had already been chosen for him. He couldn't find another to replace Usma Tahara. A path not of his own volition, but in a world full of pretty, young girls, he chose this. Since it chose him, not the other way round, he knew in his heart that given half a chance he would embrace Usma any day, and this sweet romance would ensue. However, being such a zealot and taking refuge in religion was increasingly becoming moot.

There was a certain sense of satisfaction in sacrifice, but Ruhul wouldn't rule out any misgivings of a sacrifice; there it was all, the makings and the trappings of a formulaic zealot in Godly glory. Seriously, if it wasn't for Usma he would not have explored this entirely new facet of spiritualism, which sometimes felt to him more infinite than any cloying love. God was infinite in embracing Him, rather than Usma, and gave Ruhul a slice of immortality to taste and glimpse into the stuff of life, he sought.

Minimalism was one of those nobler rarities that he acquired in celibacy. He wouldn't deny that there were moments when he thought of Usma and how she lived a placid life abroad and who didn't bother to keep in touch, not even send him an occasional postcard. He was convinced that she never felt a shred of love at all. Why? Had she protested lifting a finger? Was she even remotely remorseful? She left with the family on a calm afternoon crying on Ruhul's mother's bosom before she left the house for her new exciting life.

His subsequent decision of adopting celibacy hurt his mother who thought that there wouldn't be any grandchildren running down these corridors, but most importantly to inherit the great traditions of the house, bordering on a fractured family tree. That bothered her so much, she stopped speaking to Ruhul until he changed his mind. But Ruhul was adamant in his unfathomable love for God. Even if he did get married one day for the sake of his mother, making love to another woman was impossible, something that would defeat the purpose of celibacy; surrendering to God.

As it played out, Ruhul was also young and restless. No matter how hard he prayed, regardless of what he sought in the end, he didn't understand desires would swell in his heart. Desperately, he tried to quell them. He would even sit down and pray nafal (optional) namaaz which would calm him down for some time and seemed to be working well. At work, he made no eye contact with his female colleagues to the extent that they were beginning to cast shadows of doubt on his sanity.

Sane, he was. Ruhul was sane. Perhaps, too sane – clinical, logical to the core. At the heart of it, he had to put himself to the test. He wanted to use Usma to prove a point; to see her at least one more time face to face to determine his loyalty towards God over her. To this end, he wanted to know where she lived. To which country she moved, then he would visit her there.

Just as well, his plans were underway. One morning, as he was reciting the Holy Quran, he heard the sounds of wailing from downstairs. It flabbergasted him. He closed and wrapped the Quran in cloth on its latticed carved wooden rehal, and stepped outside of the room. Downstairs, he saw Usma's father visiting after a long fifteen years. What's wrong, Ruhul thought? As he approached him, he saw a broken man, he was so bereaved that his incoherent words could only be sensed.

Something terrible had happened to Usma. She was returning with her two girls. She had married and her husband of four years was arrested for punching a hole through the wall over a rough argument. A divorce was imminent. For the first time, Ruhul felt he was losing his balance. This sanity, which he earned over these past long years was waning. He felt he was back in his kingdom again, being a King ruling it with Usma by his side.

_____

First published by *Alien Buddha Zine* #53, Alien Buddha Press, USA, 2023

Burnt Omelette

It was an uncannily quiet afternoon. I felt like water sodden dead log as I walked to the summer cottage through the Whittle Thorn forest near our house, within the suburbia of Whittle Thorn. Moments ago, I heard in a news report an abduction in the suburb. Surrealistic, how some news sunk in without having any effect whatsoever, other than this parched feeling at the back of the tongue on a scorched afternoon sun. But I kept walking through the forest. A whipping bird lashed out as I slowed. I felt a whip crack my back. It did not bring a tear to my glass eye. They were a dry desert, prickly as cactus. I rubbed them a couple of times, I wish something would rub off from being with the best ones. They were the best, I tried to hang out with in their tranquil hangout.

A man ushered me into a cottage that smelt of burnt toast and burnt egg omelette. Nothing in this cottage could shepherd the delight of surging romance, a notion. Barren was not how I felt; it was a feeling of a much deeper sense of being abandoned. An abundance of hatred filled my heart from treachery and betrayal. This man whom I called "Uncle" when I looked upon him as an "Uncle". He shredded my childhood, and put me through a paper shredder. As I recalled that other afternoon, I was at his place. Obedience was not in dearth, around the clock that was all I did. Obey, and followed him around the house until he broke. Hunger and lust cascade like ink out of a bottle. Real ink, who saw it these days, anyway? I did. I saw how his eyeliners darkened, painted with sooty coatings of coal ink. He grabbed me. I blinked and passed out.

When I woke up, it was evening. Bodily pains and shivers ran through my spine. I saw a diminishing sun over the horizon. Heavy like a dead log, I felt no remorse until I stood up and felt it, the blues between my thighs. Doors were open and I saw a few men. Jabbering away, one looked my way, I heard about the abduction then. Played the part, I was burning up, Uncle had a round head scar which I saw for the first time. With all the other men, he too was listening to the news of abduction. Play the part? What part was he playing? In the heart of it, I lay low and waited for my chance. I wished I'd had a crowbar.

Uncle entered the room and looked me in the eye.

Oh, how could you? You heinous son of a bitch, how could you do this? You heard me, I said out loud in my mind, those lousy moments as I glared back at him in silence as always, waiting for the next instruction. Instrumental to this abduction, Uncle took me under his wings after I became orphaned. Courage failed me and I waited it out, for my turn to avenge. Uncle held me by my shoulder as he walked me to the cottage. Others didn't. What more could they do to me, I thought.

Despicable people had vulnerability, and hubristic in thinking that no evil could touch them. Of course not, because they were all evil themselves. Evil upon evil upon evil, compounded to make a hot air bubble of ever-growing evils, when one day the bubble had to burst.

The cottage smelt of what it did: burnt toast and burnt egg omelette. Heaps of other kinds of smells entwined the space. Cocaine and alcohol staled the air, to say the least. Concern was how to smell the fresh air, still, and feel free. This was claustrophobic. Uncle's gang was here already. They were planning something big. Uncle was hiding in plain sight all this while, playing a double part of a benevolent elder, deceptive and whimsical. It was now clear. I sighed, but I was not resigned and I looked for ways to get out of this. Burnt toasts and omelette. This wasn't enough. There had to be dust storms and coal dust spatters; inhale to make lungs a perforated organ full of holes, I somewhat prayed. I was out of my wits.

Uncle sat me down in a chair while he negotiated with his gang. They were selling me out to the highest bidder, while oil was heating on the puny cottage stove for more omelette. My prayers were answered. I saw a hole in the cottage floor. An object was flashing a shine to my glass eye. I picked it up when no one was looking. Sharp as a razor blade, I kept it in my fist. When a child was born it entered the world with its fist closed; it held a one-way ticket to the blue. This razor was that ticket. I began to cut myself, I screamed until they noticed. They couldn't sell damaged goods.

Blood flowed from the cuts but they bandaged every one of those wounds, while Uncle negotiated in the other room. I lay alone for a bit, then jumped blindly through an open window like a petrified kangaroo. Uncle hadn't counted on this; I had lost some blood and they thought I was weak. Boom. Boom. Boom, I heard gunshots coming my way; I made it to a darkly dense hedge. Camouflaged in the forest, I hid myself well amongst the browns of its plains. Charming as it was, the cottage could have been a safe house but it only housed crooks like Uncle.

The party was over, or I hoped it would be soon, but people still hopped around, lurking; my heart was thumping. I feared there were more, more like me, at risk. At least, I knew the Uncle's hideout if I could get away I would burn the whole house down. Night owls came out of the woods, and sat on high branches, I wasn't, not yet. Still, hiding away from the ubiquitous dance of spotlights through the forest. One of the owl's hoots instilled in me some hope, the highways were close, and I knew, If I made it through this if I could somehow get to the highway soon.

Something was burning again. It trickled through my nostrils. Not more burnt omelette. Smoke was rising over the cottage, a spark there must have started a fire that was devouring trees and the forest denizens. More and more torches were snuffed out, useless against this fire's luminous forces. Caught up in this towering inferno, the cottage was burnt down to a cinder too, with everyone in it before they even knew what struck them or how – raging, engulfing, a breathing dragon, and I? I was already in the firm clasps of the owl's solid toes, as it towed me away. The party was over soon. It seriously was.

———————

First published by *Ink Pantry Curator of Fine Words*, UK, 2023

City Smell

Dimly lit under the street lamps in an old alley at midnight, a nostalgia wells up. A perceptible city smell tickles the nostrils in humidity fuelled singed heat. Yeah, the lamps bestow light on the strays lying down on empty alleys – clean, and silent as the rains wash away any debris otherwise invisible to the naked eye, slants through the midnight street lamp – dark, heavy, and blue. To an ever-wakening and heightened sensory perception, a city sleeps, unhinged like exposed skeletons.

The city smells, however, another smell pushing through the winds and more pervasive, makes breathing hard; terrified barks and human squeals tear up the skies. The rains are gone now but smoke burns rise in the atmosphere, buckets drop cling-clang on the ground in haste; sirens of fire trucks, and a few explosive sounds. The strays stop barking. Squeals are quiet too. The burning dissipates. Silence descends; the city smell crawls back, buried into the ground.

First published by *Mad Swirl*, USA, 2024

84

In Stillness

Well then? What did it matter whether she was living or dead? My mother's pictures were strewn across the iPhone screen like innumerable stars in a night sky. When I viewed them, they looked exactly the same as the ones who were still living that I had not visited in ages. In stillness, it didn't matter. They all looked alike. Dead or alive, still pictures of whatever image is carved out of them. What if just for the sake of argument, I placed this picture of a living person right beside that of a dead person? Stilly still – both dead to me or alive. A trick, my imagination played – stirred up an impossible emotion to let me believe that my mother was living and well, just like the living person's picture beside hers. Her picture beside my mother's made no difference; they both looked exactly the same. Not any state-of-the-art special credence was given for being alive, but to the contrary. Well, let me be beguiled then, by my imagination, so I may stand up to death – a ruse I had established to alternate reality of still photographs. Believe what you want to believe. Believe it or not, I will elude you – death. I viewed the two pictures on my screen one dead, the other alive. I believed what was before me. I believed they were both alive – no more, no less.

_____

First published by *The Alien Buddha Skips the Party Part Two, Introspective Anthology,* Alien Buddha Press, USA, 2022

Collector's Item

Bones remembered. They read like an open story book. Of creatures, of habits, of cultures; if bones were to be reconstructed and retraced, a narrative of a forgotten race could emerge like a dancing dream. In my deep sleep who I dreamt of was no more predictable or consequential than my skin-deep complexion. Just as well, the face I dreamed last night was inconsequential and unpredictable. Yet, I dreamed of someone in my unconscious, subterranean self; I dreamed a hobbit slammed a door to my face in not so subtle ways.

I know this hobbit; I've known him for years. Who often chided me, laughed at my button nose and the dark tone of my skin. Until one day, I literally stepped on his toes for being churlish. He was in the throes of a maddening mid-life crisis, and I, in my sweet twenties. I grumbled, I was grim, his grimy comments tormented me; he told me that I had a pig-nose, that I was the black baby of this fair-skinned family, without any hope of ever securing a husband. *Who would marry me?* Thankfully, I wasn't the black sheep, because I had the graciousness to repeatedly forgive him for his rudeness. I was better than him. He was such a tease!

Well-groomed, the hobbit harboured a desire to become king. He was our neighbour's grandson. Growing up, he pulled my pigtails an awful lot. I never took him seriously, particularly his waywardness affected me. I realised that but I was also helpless to avoid him because he would be everywhere – by the lake, barking up the same or the wrong tree, too, sometimes which I also did, in the forests, the mountains peaks, the old haunts as it were; as though he could read my mind. As though he timed me and he knew exactly where to find me.

Liked him? I did not for calling me black, button-nosed creature of the night. But what could I do? When I tried telling an adult, they ignored me, laughed it away, calling me a button-nosed *Krishna* as well – the dark girl. I heard it so often being called the "dark beauty", the "dark night", even "dark knight", that the word "dark" sunk into me like a stinging fly as a tell-tale sign of the adults grinning at me like Cheshire.

The suspicions began to stir my sensibilities; a confusion arose within me as to the use of that adjective – elevated me sometimes as one who possessed exuberant "dark beauty" or lowly condescension to "dark ugly". Nice try. But my fortitude and optimism quelled such misgivings, and gave me the strength to rise above such double-edged sarcasms/compliments, apportioned by the adults.

I stood tall, lifted my brows and held a button-nose high as I went about my way, bracing myself from any negativity seeping into me. I was a beacon of resilience. I began to laugh with them. My family fed me well, took me to the best forests, told me the best fantasies about our elves and fairies. I listened to the best flute music and vocals. My cave-room was full of rarest forest flowers, and gifts of precious gems, rubies, lapis lazuli, and diamonds glittered, everywhere I looked. My family taught me well, to be fearless and proud.

The hobbit spent an awful lot of time with my family and me. His mind soaking up all the toxicity around my looks. While I had a clear plan as to what I wanted in life, he had none, and often floundered in the most wicked dreams. When he teased me about my looks, I also played along laughing and gave back some in banter; fruitless and impervious as he was to a purposeless life. While I wanted to be a healer, he? Well, king of *terra nallius*. For he was

87

just that – king of nobody who only excelled in churlish behaviour.

No wait, not entirely. He did have some interests. Because one afternoon, I walked over to his grandfather's big cave next door, I entered, not a soul was in or around. I entered a library full of all kinds of dead species, birds, insects. Some rare butterflies, also, dreadfully pinned against the cave skirt walls. Stuffed animals of hunted tigers, speared lion heads, and curved elephant tusks. Grandfather and Great, Great, Grandfathers spared no animals in all the jungles as they went about their infamous hunting and gathering ruse without compunction. They literally looted the nearby forests, and left nothing for other hobbits.

Looking at these, I wondered what else they collected. I ventured upstairs to the other rooms. Trespassing? Sure it was, but I have been walking these great halls forever, too, never this far though, not even the library, always closed. The hobbit's bedroom doors were ajar, just when I heard footsteps at the entrance downstairs. He entered with a folded bark under his arm. I retreated deeper into the dark walls.

He ascended the jagged stairs, two rapid steps at a time, and went into his room. The door was still wide open. I heard dropping noise. I peeked from behind him and saw some bones rolling out of the bark as it unfolded. Were they hobbit or animal bones I had no idea? I came out of my hiding, and descending the stairs, I fast paced through the mountain passes, back into our cave next door. It was my deep secret, I discreetly held within myself until I decided to find out more. I was taught to be fearless and free.

It was crazy. Why would no body be present when I was in there? Was this deliberate? I went to their cave many times, but never did I see anything like it. Did they actually want me to see those objects? I always thought they were great hunters and travellers. Whose mother died at childbirth? Whose father and grandfather raised him to be a hobbit of the world, sent him across several seas to learn more about life? Who grew up in a family without bonding to any female, who, in his spare time came to our place; a joyful cave teeming with my aunts, uncles, cousins, mum and dad with whom he bonded. Of course, me.

The hobbit never cared to speak much about anything. He was a vapid soul, an empty shell unaffected by these bones he collected. Bones belonging to those who would routinely tried to find gold in throw-away rocks after a clean dig of the hobbit owned goldmine grounds. Where such hobbits living in abject poverty would hammer away on these empty rocks in the hope of leftover gold dust, until death claimed their souls and their bodies lay scattered. No gold was ever found, or ever meant to be found in those hard rocks, except their bones.

Hard rocks. The fanciful hobbit goldmine, a deadly cesspool of exploitation where other hobbits worked themselves to death in the hope of more meat and food through the deadly hours of the dark, hot mines, honing skills for more gold out of the rocks, blood being vamped, bones being chewed until their teeth clenched, muscles relaxed, and the dwarf bodies lay pale and petrified. Bones, brought home, stripped off any traces of soft tissues, or faintest skin colour.

Down to the bare bones. Our hobbit friend suddenly died. Where they were collected and preserved in a bone library of all kinds of Neanderthal, Homo Floresiensis, Australopithecus, Paranthropus, and the earliest-known Homo Erectus skeletons, his bones, even in extinction, proved to be infinite; every inch fossilised in the purest, solid form, his tales locked in. Unlike others, I didn't have a single bad bone my mother always said. It's all in the bone. The rest were fantasies, lost in a vapour of ice.

_____

First published by *BlazeVOX Special Issue,* USA, spring, 2024

Maya

Clouds trailed crisscrossed across a clear blue sky. A cotton candy man stood by a huge Ferris Wheel with his cart at a theme park showground. He watched the Ferris Wheel move slowly to a full circle. Maya Julian stepped forward with her five-year-old and joined the long queue to get on the Ferris Wheel. Tilting her neck, she put a hand across her forehead like a vizier to cover her eyes from the blazing sun. She felt that the wheel did not move much – almost too slow for the world to be defined from the top there. Her daughter, Saira, and her, perhaps didn't look all that different from ants and moths, milling about haphazardly on the showground.

As Maya looked at the top, she didn't see any trepidation in the children or the adults. All was shipshape. The candy man attended to the many children on the ground, adeptly adjusting the pinky floss around the candy stick, and handing them over the pink dandelions in a bouquet, as it were, with a benign smile.

Children couldn't wait to mouth the pinky candy. However, the Ferris Wheel stopped moving for a while which no one else noticed except Maya, who felt nervous and felt she must alert the authorities for an alternate way to get those people down. They didn't see it coming. They sat here without a concern. Maya gathered the reason for their placidness was perhaps they couldn't see much from above.

The candy man looked up a few times like Maya. A frown appeared on his forehead too, which Maya saw, and wondered if he also noted that there was a problem. If the situation went out of hand, people could be in fatal trouble. Her daughter pulled her towards the candy cart, and they both came out of the queue losing their place in it. On her way to the cart, she saw people – mainly children with an older sibling or an adult jostling in the bottom of the wheel

91

as they dribbled out of the lower cabins of the Ferris Wheel touching the green grass beneath.

The ones at the top hung precariously, oblivious to what was coming next. The sky couldn't look clearer. The clouds spread out like a fishing net through which no fish could escape. Trapped inside the net – not until then, not really until it happened that someone dropped a net into the blue bowled ocean and trapped all these frantic fish inside it; the net teeming with all the fish out of water when life was pulled out of this oxygenated cosmic ocean into the outer. Until then calm prevailed.

Those sitting at the top, were clueless, enjoying a breezy morning – chirping and laughing spring birds. Maya trembled in the fresh air as she took her daughter to buy candy floss. The candy man continued to look at the Ferris Wheel.

"Are you thinking, what I am also thinking?" Maya asked.

"What are you thinking?" he asked.

"I think that the wheel is broken. Those who are at the top, are all stuck."

"Hmm, that's exactly what I was thinking too."

"What now?" Maya asked.

"Someone must tell the manager of this theme park, I reckon," replied the candy man.

"Do you know where his office is? I'll let him know."

The candy man looked over his shoulder and pointed towards a building at the far end of the park. Maya squinted to follow his directions. Then she took her daughter's hand and began to walk towards the management building while the decadent candy floss melted in her daughter's mouth. Maya looked at her and smiled. She smiled back.

"Where're we going Mammy?" she asked.

"To tell the manager to fix the Ferris Wheel?"

"Why? What's wrong with it?"

"It isn't working well, darling."

"Is it broken?" she asked.

"I think so," Maya replied.

"Will they all die at the top?" the daughter asked.

"No, of course not, the manager will ensure that," Maya said.

The daughter kept licking the candy cane to its bare bone until the stick was fully exposed. She looked at it and gave it a long-lasting lick, top to bottom. The manager's building was far, but Maya persevered. She stepped up, determined to stop the disaster at the Ferris Wheel at any cost. At any cost? However, when she reached the building, she found a big padlock at its gate. She pushed it and pulled the lock but it did not open. Lights in one of the rooms were on. She looked up and she screamed; strikingly close, not quite far enough. She looked around for an object and found a rock. Maya did the unimaginable. She picked it up and hurled it aiming higher at the glass window. It rocketed through the glass. Shards fell and hit Maya on her forehead. "Oh" she uttered and sat down.

The daughter looked up at the window and shook Maya by the shoulder. Maya felt an urgency in the shake and looked up too. Her jaw fell. At the window, there was a man, not even a full man, maybe a half-man and half-elf. He – it looked like a statue with inky tears running down its cheeks. This was a make-believe theme park. A rock came flying out of nowhere; it transpired into a piece of paper as it landed with just one word written – ignis fatuus.

"What does this mean?" the daughter asked.

Maya replied, "Illusion", "foolish fire".

"Isn't that what your name also means?"

The daughter wanted to know from a breathless mother.

First published in *The Chiron Literary Review Winter Issue*, USA December 2024

Rainfall in Soho

Ulfaat gazes at petrified moths through flour jars. While some are flapping wings, others are quite not. The air-tight jars make it harder to get in than out. Even with all the clever cling-wrapping securely pasted over the jars' openings, doesn't prevent infestation. Without any fear, moths gather here in death throes. She opens the lids; those who can, fly out in trepidation, happy to be released.

Her flour shop on the cul-de-sac of Soho Street can close down if a complaint is lodged. She can't sell moth-ridden flour to her customers any more than she can bread up the flour herself. Whichever way she braids the dough, the dough is spoiled one way or the other. A tinkle at the front door alerts her to a customer walking in. He asks to buy a kilo of flour. She bites her lips and disappears to the back of the store. He notices her rather long, pale face but doesn't ask.

Well, of course, she isn't going to tell him about the moths. Moth eggs may have been laid in this sack too. If any is cocooned within the sack, it's just not her day. She fetches a sack of flour to the front hoping for none to be found. The man pays and leaves. Ulfaat wonders what if inspectors come around and shut her down? What if this customer finds moths and reports her to the consumer's affairs? She sits down at the till and thinks of her baby.

No one knows when relationships go pear-shaped. One notices when poetry stops flowing. Effusive words of "oneness", "inseparable", "entwined" and "kindred spirits all take a sour turn south replaced by "do this", "do that". "What do you do around the house all day, sit on your fat ass? Years of shitty life I've had with you – you! Who couldn't follow a simple instruction – you are stupid –

bloody stupid," stings her beating heart; she suffocates under the weight of such prosaic rhetoric.

In the heart of it, poetry had blossomed once. In her twenties then, she was writing in full swing. She never thought she could ever write a book. She never thought she could flesh out flat characters right. She felt she was committing herself to an ever-doomed project. The more she wrote, the more needed to be written. She sought direction.

Just like her book, a marriage based on poetry was a mirage. One monsoon morning, after she'd bathed, she'd brushed her wet hair and let it down to her waist; she stood out on the balcony of her father's house. He lived two houses down the road. He saw her from his top-floor window. His name was Irfan. He waved through the foggy rain. The clouds descended; the winds and the rain chimed a tune, while she held on to the veranda rails and steadied herself.

He had seen her through the rains; her cascading hair of sinewy vine maple branches, wavering in the winds. As a neighbour, he might have seen her once or twice. Her subtle beauty revealed itself in the new foglight. The doorbell rang. She opened it. He stood outside. Monsoon had brought her a message – a harbinger of a sort. He was soaking wet. She asked him to come inside. "I'm writing a book," she told him.

"A book?" he asked with a frown, then kissed her pouted lips – a cigar-flavoured kiss, with a faint blend of her musky odours did all the trick. Magic was born.

Ulfaat found out later – much, much later...

By now she had married him happily one summer's day. By this time her book had been shelved, covered under many layers of cobwebs. He promised her panting heart the world. He was taking her places. She embarked on a joy ride; a full-on journey had ensued. Where to? She had asked herself. Did it matter? Not really. She would follow him to the end of the world; so be it, so be it!

She reaches the tipping point of a long struggle. Feeling accosted, she breaks down before a chilli river – a red, hot curried fish. Her runny nose and tears from onion cuts are indistinguishable from her powerlessness. He says it is delicious, perfect. But she knows it's too hot; she likes it because he likes it. She tells him that chillies don't irk her.

No, the chillies are a menace. The red, hot river is causing a dent in his intestine. The poisonous chilly river is killing him; that she is killing him; that he is struggling to chill. Why? Is there another woman then? She thinks. He must be in love with another woman – wooing, and cooing her as he had done her that monsoon night. It is the chillies, he says. She must stop this nonsense.

She stops. Chillies are a far cry, now. Her baby lies in her crib. He eats dinner another night, he asks why the curry is bland. Ulfaat tells him. He laughs out loud and says, "You crazy bitch, you think I'm not strong enough to stomach hot curry?"

Ulfaat says, "I don't know, you tell me, isn't the hot chilly drilling a hole in your stomach?"

He rises abruptly from his chair. Dinner half-eaten, he picks up his plate and drops it on the hard floor – through the many floral china shards, the bland gravy flows all over the kitchen tiles. But it doesn't stop there. He picks up a kitchen knife and lunges towards Ulfaat, who is still eating dinner. He walks up close and holds the knife around her neck. Her baby cries out; he startles and drops the knife.

Calm prevails; he reverts to his charming self. He even

asks her forgiveness and begs her to not ever to leave him. Chillies or no chillies, she thinks he has condemned her, one way or another. Her formidable husband irks her more than the menacing chillies. She nurses the baby. The baby has colic. The husband has a hole. Ulfaat stands steadfast in between to reach a goal.

One night Irfan doesn't return. Ulfaat sits by the window feeding her colic baby. She has an early start the next morning. The case of moth infestation in the jars is resolved. The old supply chain has to be cut. Fresh flour is arriving at her shop in the morning through a new supplier. The phone rings at three AM. Irfan's frantic voice asks her to come to the local police station.

Three AM, Ulfaat picks up her sleeping baby and walks into the police station up the road. A man is injured in a brawl. He is recovering in the hospital. Fingers point at Irfan, who beat him up in a bar. He is looking at a month at least in prison time unless the charges are dropped.

She needs a Genie – a pop-out sprite of goodness from someplace – lamp, bottle, jar, or whatever.

Irfan has a mental disorder, most likely, schizophrenia. His mind needs to clear the vile melancholia. The injured man is better. He drops the charges when he hears of sickness inflicting Irfan. Psychiatric care is given to Irfan before his release from prison.

A reasonable man, Ulfaat's Genie, appears at her shopfront one rainy evening. This man stirs an odd emotion in her heart and her gut. Fresh sacks of moth-free wheat and mud-red rice flour arrive early morning. He buys a sack of red, rice flour. On his way out he turns around, and winks at Ulfaat, and then he grins. She doesn't let her sadness steal her smile. She brings her best, a bold smile to her lips, to which he nods and steps out. He plods along the wet parking lot. The rainfall can't be sweeter on her Soho block.

First published in *Porchlight Literary Review*, Indonesia, January 2024

Somersaulting the Seaweed

Elements

Seaweed tonic balms the skin; the precious ingredients are locked in. Pores close as soon as the body is taken out of a warm bath and exposed to cold. Air.Water.Earth.Fire is locked into the skin of the universe's porous pores, hot first, cool next. The stuff of life, Air.Water.Earth.Fire is eternally floating, and cooking seaweed broth in a hotpot. The broth consists of rare spices such as crying, laughing, dancing, dreaming, creating, inventing, wavering, dying, recycling, and awakening in an exhilarating range of riveting gauges. Propagating, loving, trilling, and killing in a fruitful and fruitless chase. Tucked away into the universe's skin, elements bring flirtatious seaweed and flitting mead.

I Fly

The air in the closed room smells like a two-day-old wash in a laundry machine. My mother tells me to open the windows to let some fresh air in. I don't budge much, except perhaps, change my sitting position. My phone rings in my hand. It's Sammy the cobbler's son. I ignore it, but the calls persist. I switch my phone off. Mother looks at me with a frown. I ignore that too. I am sick of Mother's pressuring gaze, do this, do that. I fly, I dive, into a braided seaweed mat.

God's Land

Space is void. Also, where I live, breathe, stand, and eat crap. I hold hands in someone else's shared space. When a third person comes along, enters into my space, and tries to push me out of it, they violate it. They are in my space sending me to someone else's space which then I violate. Violating each other's space like a falling domino. Space belongs to all; it belongs to no one. Space is coveted, negotiable, and teeming with life, squeezing into each other's territory, creatures become territorial, aggressive, and mercenary. Yet, space is fluid, but an ocean full of sweet seaweed; of pixies, of fairies frolicking on a bed of relics.

Optical Illusion

Jars of lemon pickle stand abreast on a store's shelf. One summer midmorning, my dad and I, with his friend Sadat, take off down a blind alley belting by my grandfather's rose garden. We exit the house and walk around the bend where the alley ends. In the midmorning sun, the pickles in the oil pale, to look syrupy white to our naked eyes, roshogollahs, specifically. We buy one each. Mouths watering, we shove 'em up straight whole onto the tongues; sugared they are not; red seaweeds on the beach are an illusory stinging jellyfish.

Fallen through the Cracks

Who is there to root for Misha? Not a speculative question when Misha thinks about it. He does not live in his birthplace but has lived many years in someone else's birthplace. He sees how the mates he hangs out with, lift each other's spirits. How they go to great lengths to sing praises of each other for success. This happens both here and there. Misha also roots for both nations' men and women. His self-esteem drops, when no one roots for him. Invisible to the eye, seaweed slides down the seaside like a gothic moonbeam glide.

The Cheat

The man has issues, thinks Payela, the neighbour girl. It isn't what he wants from her, love. But how he wants it in secrecy, so his wife wouldn't know about it. A wife who deprives him of love, in his wedded life. He thinks he is in love with the neighbour girl. That this love is divine. A need that only she can meet – his ultimate salvation. He begs for it. He cries for it. Deprived as he is, the neighbour girl doesn't trust him. She refuses. Seaweed crawls, completely in her thrall, he sings no more *trall*.

Blunt Blade

Blunt cut on green papaya difficult as it is, Sarwat takes it up as a challenge to test endurance. With all her physical strength, she digs the knife deep through the papaya's tough, green veneer, until the knife comes out on the other end; until papaya slices and halves. Now the peeling begins. The knife is quite blunt; she cleans the milky, slippery sap. Seaweed Lamina dances to a beach rap; Sarwat sluices her face with water from the tap. The blade slides down the skin in bitesize; sweat beads push through her forehead. She dabs them off with a kitchen rag and persists until all of the greens are blown. To put it bluntly, the cuts are blunt, but her mettle is clearly shown.

Mother's Room

I still call it that, Mother's Bedroom. As I lie on a lazy afternoon in that room, her bed, I hear Mother's recital of a long poem. Written by Tagore, Mother is laughing and chatting about him, and his profound philosophy on life and death. Death is not an end, but a gateway to eternity where all grim reality ends. Death is done as more deaths occur "die, die" until death itself is dead; seaweed slithers, I close my eyes and open them in this curtained dark room, where Mother is meant to be. I see a white wall right next to me. I see a pink bob face appear through the wall; this painted young girl then disappears into one of the four corners of the room. I lay here. Wide open eyes, in Mother's Room on this lazy afternoon where her hot breath is entombed.

Journey's End

Immersion in hot seaweed juices, and cold sluices in the aftermath, work like magic on young skin. Only when the skin is not yet broken by the elements Air.Water.Earth.Fire is collectively active to keep the skin green, up until it is akin to a grandmother's octogenarian. Life events continuously change: shifting sands and moonbeam tricks. All in good time, when history repeats, reality becomes fantasy. Today's reality, is yesteryear's fantasy, a throwback into the past, like a dream. The present poses a threat to time, another cyclical fantasy. Air.Water.Earth.Fire harvests seaweed again to bring slimy sheen akin to silken new skin.

_____

First published in *DarkWinter Literary Magazine*, Canada, May 2024

Cage

He sits in his dark room like a caged beast. Only a window is his opening to the outer world. His interaction with birds and flowers satisfy him. No one chains him as such. A master of everything he beholds, his world isn't small in his isolation until one day, he hears a song, not the singer, is when he feels passionate to seek her. The melody knocks him over; he realises that he has a life and what's he misses by not being out there. However, when he rises to go out, he cannot.

First published by *RIC Journal*, Bangalore/Paris, January 2024

Ghazal

I only remember the last two lines.

Humming them repeatedly, rummaging through my memory to find the whole song.

I wish to remember it, to sing it all.

But I must contend myself with a partial two-line because the rest is history.

What I hum all day is, "heart's desires always remain unfulfilled, where are you, where are you, my love?"

The more I sing, the more abundant is the yearning; the more the broken lines beckon me to sing again.

Engulfing a part of me; until the lines become me like the mourning Electra – enduring; forever searching; forever restive.

First published in *RIC Journal, Bangalore/Paris,* January 2024

Fire

In a jaundiced sky, bats and crows flew amok in uncertain directions at dusk. The sky, a canvas of black jittery spots, to behold from the space above. A blaze over the tall gum trees was a tell-tale sign, suggesting the end of time. The fire grew. The creatures of the forest, the possums, the dingoes, and the Tasmanian tigers, the denizens of the forest ran deeper around the bend. Distant cries of human voices carried distress. Trees and houses and the animal habitat, all burnt to a cinder. The fire burnt without ebb, without a reprieve. A permanent haze descended from the sky; it darkened the forest. Luminous fire sparks, but like ubiquitous fireflies bejewelled a feral frontier. A pegged male and a female pants blew in the hot winds on a singed clothesline. They landed on each other. A magpie swooped, sat sentinel for a while. Its curiosity piqued; regurgitated and beaked, as the fire raged.

First published in *Terror House Magazine*, USA, March 2020

Liquid Doll

Sulaiman and his friend Omar were rummaging through dolls at a doll store looking to buy a perfect doll for Sulaiman's five-year-old niece, Hamza.

"Where is this promised land I keep hearing about all around me? What sort of a place is this?" Sulaiman asked.

Omar looked at him and shrugged.

They searched through a selection of dolls, in minis, middies and long flowing skirts, hijab, and without. Through blonds, brunettes, black hair, and white. None would satisfy.

"What kind of doll does she like?" Omar asked. "Perhaps, that could give us some directions, rather than this clueless search for the perfect doll."

"I don't know, the kind that wouldn't melt in a desert sun," Sulaiman laughed. "The last one I bought her melted in the dune by the time I gave it to her."

"How did that happen?" Omar asked.

"I was stuck in a desert storm with the doll in my sack."

"Pity! What a pity?" Omar chuckled.

"At that moment, I also had a strange vision that my mother's dehydrated dead body had been submerged in a fountain of youth. When her body was hydrated enough, it was taken out, and the water was shaken off, it transformed into the body of a teenager; new life was infused into her. She became a young woman, full of life. Perfect, but in the form of a living doll."

"Could she speak, dance, and skip?" Omar asked.

"Yes, she could do all those again, and more. This life was forever, But it was doll-like, somewhat." Sulaiman answered.

"What do you mean, "doll-like?" Omar asked.

"As I recall, I had called her in my vision. It was a long-distance trunk call. I felt a trepidation inside – a mad rush to see her," Sulaiman said.

"What did she tell you, though?" Omar asked.

"She said that I couldn't, because she was in the land of the dolls where she lived and breathed, but she was also tied to a visible string. I wasn't allowed here. The vision was strange."

"I'd say," Omar said, who didn't understand.

The two friends sat abreast on a bench before all the beautiful dolls, at the doll store, They held several of them in their hands too, both tall and short, blue, brown, and black-eyed dolls in blue tight slacks. But they bought nothing. Eventually, they rose and stepped out of the store. Sulaiman looked concerned that he couldn't find the perfect doll for his niece.

His camel dug its lanky four legs into the deep sand grains; a black storm rose in the desert, gusts blew the dust around, and sands rolled in; they covered the sky. The doll was in a sack on the camel's back, melting, even as we spoke. He sat here watching the dense storm; his head and face were covered with a long, checked scarf. In the thick of it, his vision of his mother returning to life, but as a puppet was clear. When the storm passed, the dunes became undeterred, seamless as they were. But the plastic doll he had bought for his niece had melted: sunken eyes, sagging cheeks, crooked nose, lopsided lips, colours dripping down its shrinking feet. A liquid mass of plastic; not a single drop of water in the desert. The storm lasted long; he couldn't gauge the exact time.

He performed his prayers in the dune as some sands slid sideways. The sun was setting down over a high sandy horizon; a southern star blinked; he took a leaching date from one of his pant pockets, chewed it and spitted out the pit on his palm which he then shoved back into the pocket. Back up on his camel he rode for another quarter of an hour; the camel's footprints littered and dimpled up a marked dune track. It stopped after a while at a red, mud-door house with a dome-red roof up against a hill. He heard women's voices indoors and footsteps scurrying up and down. Until they came out. A few of them stood at the door, others stood outside. They greeted him with ululation. He got off his camel; they came forward to kiss him on his cheeks, then led him inside.

Sulaiman didn't know that the doll had pulverised. However, when he went inside and sat on the cushioned carpet in the living room, he opened his bag. To everyone's dismay, they found that he was holding a liquid doll. Hamza was sitting close by, looking eagerly, but shrieked in fear and broke down in tears at the decapitated doll before her; her longing for dolls, dissipating. Everyone tried to calm her down. But Hamza was inconsolable. Lambs, too began to bleat frantically outside the mud walls. Sulaiman told her that he was sorry, but it wasn't over. All this happened because of the long wait in the hot sun and a dusty, desert storm. These things happened in life, noting that nothing was *really* set in stone.

The lambs were still bleating in his mind as he sat with his friend Omar outside a glassed cubicle at the doll store. Where was this promised land? One melted doll in the high desert sun. Mother was old when she died. But she rose again and became a laughing, walking, talking living doll, even loving like a sweet sixteen in one of the allies. Here he was with his friend, Omar, to buy another doll. That would've been pleasing if he could, yet he could not choose one.

Satin sands slipped through his fingers in the storm.

Heavenly bodies move on the far side of the dunes; the sun drops and the moon rises. A sun also dropped in the doll land. But much more benign than the sun which melted Hamza's liquid doll. A persuasive sun that rejuvenated dolls.

Couldn't he buy her another doll from the store? Couldn't he keep his promise? He was wrong, wrong all along; some things *were* set in stone in these strictly parametric worlds.

First published by *Argyle Literary Review, USA, 2024*

The Yellow God

Elves, Fairies, and little Pixies gather at a tea party amongst the sprinkling stars. Cupcakes made of moon drops and grassroots are served, kebabs made of mashed passion fruits and sweet persimmon, glazed bushberry sandwiches from box elder tree sap trickles. Pixie lord Glunaag declares that each elf and fairy must sing or dance. A dance floor must be prepared.

At his behest, Pixies construct a dance floor. They transform themselves into frozen tears. And create a serene riverine dance floor in a far-side lunar crater. On its completion, sprites begin their intrepid, sprightly dances on the ice river surface; they fly, twist, swing, and flap their translucent, ethereal wings. They dance along with the orchestrated chorus sung by silver birds. Afterwards, every frozen teardrop cracks up to let out each pixie back into its fluorescent body. However, one pixie drops a tear by chance onto an African tulip in the woodlands; a single teardrop cups the secret of lush crops; grains, teeming with vitality and life are a gift of the bountiful sprites.

Guests gather at a community hall for a wedding on Tallow Beach this pale afternoon. A bride and a groom covered in turmeric paste on their *Haldi* ceremony – a prelude to their wedding – sit on a dais. An arching rainbow veers in and out between layers of clouds.

At the Haldi, Mother with her mate Juniper organise ceremonial flowers and view the rainbow's movements of entries and exists. Juniper tells her, "There are invisible water droplets behind the rainbows, making them appear as this colourful band in the sky. While the water drops remain hidden to the eye, the hues are droplets imparted through the sun – transcendence in nature."

Haldi ceremony is age-old. This tradition spans over five thousand years and passes down many generations. Today, though, it lasts only for a few hours. As it turns out turmeric has skin replenishing quality. It cleanses oil and dirt deposits, and makes the skin glow; the essential goodness and the yellow colour are its limitless intrinsic properties – God knows, the sky is the limit. Hence, the bride and the groom are bathed in the turmeric liquid for a new beginning. They wear the venerable yellow mask, and leave it for an hour or so until it dries. Until they rub it off gently for all the dirt and the oil to wash away for the skin to exfoliate and brighten for a complete makeover to happen.

Mother diligently grinds some turmeric paste into a mortar and pestle, then plops the paste into a silver bowl. She places the bowl on a silver platter. When the ceremony begins, each guest carries the silver platter and walks to the duo to apply a puny smoothy onto the groom's and the bride's forehead. A betel leaf is used as a scoop. Guests scoop some paste on the leaf's pointy tip and wipe the paste off on the couple's forehead and face. Splashes of the paste drop on their bridal clothes, too. Turmeric yellow is a stubborn stain to remove. The bride has a dark, red silk skirt, and the groom has a yellow silk top.

For all intents and purposes, the bride decides how she wishes to wed. Mother is happy that she has chosen well. Romance must prevail at any cost. Neither the groom nor Mother wants any clash over traditions. Mother encourages her son to comply with the bride's wishes. As it is, it is widely known that turmeric is endowed with phytonutrients, also beneficial in Ayurveda for relieving arthritic pains and other remedies that cannot be undermined either medically or poetically, this magical ceremony.

The cloud clears up on the Tallow. A straight narrow lane of sun ray tears through the window curtains of the community hall; an infinitesimal dust plume floats in the light's pathway. The ray fills up the room full of flowers. As guests mill about, Juniper crouches on the floor and appears to be collecting some petals dropped off a white gardenia, and tries to reattach them to the flowers' unadorned stem head. Juniper is flustered that he can't redo the petals. He leaves them scattered all over the floor and runs to re-join the ceremony. However, he doesn't find anyone here. The room is empty – no decorations, no cheering crowds; only a steady pathway laid out by the golden sun.

Blue room. Juniper sees a baby cot. He rushes towards it but he slips on a wooden floorboard. The cot beckons him. A patched-up quilt hangs down its tall crib bars. A baby sleeps in blue sleepers. Mother enters the room. She carries the baby to wake it up for the next cuddle feed. When the telephone also rings – a red wired phone plugged into a wall socket. She puts the baby back into the crib and walks over to take the call.

"What nonsense." All she hears is the chugged noise of a boat through the speaker. Mother lets the handset drop hanging it by the phone, and returns to attend to the baby's needs, who is awake and cries out loud. Trepidation swells within her gut as she hears the cry. Chugging along through the handset, she does not heed the sound, but covers the baby with a light blue blanket, and offers it her breast. Baby's cheeks are flushed with red.

A midsummer afternoon sun burns at the planet's core. Its flaring particle can fry an egg on a rock's rugged crust. The baby settled and nourished, Mother puts it back into the crib. Juniper hears Father's voice from an ocean in the backdrop of dolphins frolicking over the waves. Dolphins are man's best friends. They rescue frenzied, drowning people and swim them to safety. Father's fishing troller capsizes in the storm. The helm is wrecked in the ferocity of the wild winds. Father is all wrapped up in the rolling waves when a dolphin tracks him. It carries him on its back and swims to a nearby shore – the island of Crete in Greece. Dolphin is spot on in its nautical assessment of the oceanic chart.

Father survives. He is given a second chance at life – God's gift. But Mother smokes out a new challenge. Father is increasingly difficult to cope with. Because he is mostly livid and dangerous; adrenaline disorders trigger hypomanic behaviour in him. The baby is nestled within the cosy comforts of the cushioned crib. Father yells out to Mother to bring him a bottle and whip. Mother obeys and brings him both; a crack of the whip on Mother's back because she brings the whiskey late. Mother cries in pain as she forges a defence against him. He also battles a bottled disease in his brain.

She cries today. But a teenage boy unlatches a door and enters into the room. He catches the whip mid-air before it can land on Mother's scarred back again. Now the boy will be whipped for stopping Father. She screams out in fear, "Run! Boy run! Latch the door on your way out!" The boy is petrified. Father is manic, right now. He can barely stand up. Mother cries out. "Run, baby, run, save yourself… go… fates… who writes them, anyway… this diseased man… I'm tethered to his whip… but you aren't boy… run, run." The boy screams back. "No, you aren't tied to his whip, either… bloody hell, it's in your head."

Time is running out for Father. He is not that strong, anymore. Father glares at the boy and clutches onto the fiery whip. He swaggers his body as he moves towards them, and both the boy and Mother wait sweating and panting for his next morbid move. He lunges at the boy, but the whip wags weakly in his hand before his arms slump to his sides. Father takes a few uneven steps back and collapses on the floor. He puts a hand to his chest, still clings to the whip. His facial colour changes from black to purple-blue; his eyeballs bulge and his mouth hangs like caricatured fractured jaws.

Father is rushed into the hospital as his heart plays up. He stays there as long as time permits until sirens find him one midnight and steal off his last few breaths, dry. A fisherman's burial is on the seabed where new life is spun. The whip is burnt to a cinder. The boy takes Mother's hand and they both move out of the house. Mother sighs in grief and relief. Another place, another time, a new place for Mother. New headspace for the boy who slowly turns into a man. Mother awaits a bold, promising future.

At the dinner table, the man is engrossed in grooming a robot which he boots and reboots. He makes it speak a natural language. Mother understands it. Mother is infirm from age, but she still cooks. The robot is seated next to him in a chair. It does not eat. Mother smiles at the robot and starts eating dinner with her son. "Get married, will you?" Mother asks of the son. With a playful smile on his wet lips, he nods that he will. But he must fall in love first. Mother looks at the robot and says, "I wish, I had a robot for a husband, but then, I wouldn't have you, would I?" The man laughs and replies. "No, you wouldn't. Without me, there wouldn't be this robot, either. One cannot exist without the other, right? Rarely, anyway." Mother smiles. Dinner finishes, shortly.

Mother wakes up in her bedroom early morning. She senses a touch and reaches out for her torch under the pillow. Last night's robot from dinner is in the room applying ointment to her discoloured skin. "What? You?"

114

Mother asks. The robot replies evenly, "Yes." "Why would you do this?" Mother asks. "Because you deserve better," it replies and then lies down beside Mother in bed. Mother is confused. But, she doesn't ask it to leave. In the morning, when she wakes up the robot is gone. She wakes up alone in an empty bed, "Fancy having a robot for a husband without the whip." She laughs at her fantasy.

Mother puts on her robe as she comes out into the kitchen area. She finds robots of all sizes – small, medium, and big. Some with breasts, even. They talk a language that only they understand. Mother observes them. Her son appears and gives her this surreptitious smile, then he walks away. Mother wonders what's all the fuss is about. Why so many robots? Has he turned this house into a robot thinking lab?

Robots don't fly into a rage. They don't have such emotions. Adrenaline doesn't flow through those artificial brain wires they aren't endowed with a frontal cortex, unlike the organic brainwaves. Mother comprehends them as machines incapable of suffering chemical imbalance, which works fine for her. However, last night's robot with his healing touch makes an impression on Mother.

Machines make breakfast. Mother doesn't even move a finger but sits crossed-legged at the table. She watches them finish the tasks; fried eggs, toast, and tea breakfast is ready. Last night's robot, shiny and yellow, crisp as the new day, brings her a tray. Mother says, "Thank you," it replies with a smile. "Welcome, I'm Juniper, the evergreen." Mother chuckles.

Chemical imbalance or not, Father's behaviour cannot be condoned. Robots seem more sentient in comparison Mother realises that life is not to give away. Without joy, life isn't worth living. But she is also afraid of change knowing full well that change is inevitable. She makes a quick foray into the future and back. She waits patiently for her son to marry, all in good time. What if they too don't find real happiness? A shiver runs through her.

Mother knows from Juniper that the rainbow's water droplets appear as a band of hues. Dolphin is an "Angel" within an aquatic mammal; Mother deems such phenomena as transcendental, they impress upon her as being mind-blowingly "real". Infinite, because while the water droplets and Angels are so, they themselves pave the way to the finite existence of rainbow colours, and carcass-melting dolphins.

The man gets married today. A much-anticipated wedding ensues following a grand Haldi ceremony. The next day top to toe bejewelled, the bride in a bright mauve skirt and a top, and the groom, in a bright red shirt and matching pants walk together around a fire – *swaha* or *agni* – for eternal bliss. The fire is ignited in a cast iron pit bowl. The couple walks around the fire seven times vowing to serve each other as husband and wife for seven generations. Mother watches with glee, how the wedding is panning out for eternity is a time-bending moment.

Elements: earth, water, fire, and wind ally to facilitate the wedding, this evening. The fire doesn't go out anytime soon but continues to grow and purifies the relationship as undiluted happiness awaits them. The priest pours purified butter, ghee to keep the flame rising. It extinguishes only after the wedding is over. However, a hitch occurs, and causes the man to pause the ceremony, because the bride is tired from the rounds. He excuses himself, by saying to his guests that the bride feels faint, and leaves the wedding stage after her – "Be back in five," he whispers to Mother. Mother shakes her head. She has faith in her son's judgment. He isn't a rainbow maker; rainbows elude her.

Father isn't here, a mere phantom; she too will become one – invisible. Juniper asks Mother to watch a hologram with him: Night falls over a rock quarry on this starry dome. A dark bride, this real beauty floats around in the hologram, and rises to dance in foggy delight: a dance with colours. Turmeric has been central since the inception of human civilisation. Another ancient fire crackles up in the quarry of this far-flung repository, a tale of a bride, and a groom unwind. The bride mesmerises Mother. She hears a whiff of her laughter through spacetime.

A child makes little boats with brittle papers and sets them assail on an unsettling rainwater puddle. She grows up into her, this dark beauty and falls in love. At her Haldi, she smells the flowers and garlands from the wedding; she hears chirrups from her forest hut and watches the celestial sights of the moon, and the blinking stars with her lover on blue nights. As the end game draws in, she envisages dimming lights on the celestial bodies of the same universe's brimming sights; the colour-dance dissolves in a blink and rapidly runs into a sinkhole of oblivion.

While the dazzling "Invisibles" – the transcendental grain-makers remain unfettered by time, unmarked by past, present, and future, the naughty, nutty fairies – the "Irreals" well and truly blindside earthlings with a sizzling mirage of a fanciful, notional "real", in which the concept of "solid" is sullied by fluid fantasy of paradox, Mother inuits from perusing life's events where the solid flesh of youth age and perish before they even know it. Life crumbles and disappears into the depths of nothingness; millions, even billions of well-grounded years, upend in three short days.

Mother's face falls. The happiness she seeks is rare; this wedding, is the only plausible ruse in her view to get her son there, to be happy. In a moment, the bride and the groom return in good spirits. Juniper, stays close to Mother. The ceremony restarts, and continues for another half hour. They are married. Now they are husband and wife. The groom can't stop smiling. Neither can the bride – stop smiling, a bit much Mother thinks – such a perfect smile, what a doll. They both shake hands with guests. Mother blesses them, her son, and his wife. The bride's delicate beauty – her sharp nose, her intense dark eyes, her arched rainbow eyebrows, and her chiselled cheeks – charm Mother.

Off to honeymoon, Juniper is with Mother at her son's instructions; Juniper is to stay with Mother and attend to all her needs. He will be back soon with his newly wedded wife. Mother hugs him. However, as she proceeds to hug his bride, her gorgeous daughter-in-law, Juniper stops her. Mother's hands are in Juniper's tight grips. Mother is shocked, and struggles in vain to pull her locked hand from its brawny bind. Juniper looks at her and says:

"Bride's Name?"
Genesis .01

"I am?"
Juniper, the evergreen

I'll give you a real name, Mother. And man, a real name, too.

First published by *Aphelion: Webzine for Science Fiction and Fantasy*, Australia, 2024

Thin Wall

Forget-me-not dear father. Please do not look at me blankly or ask who I am. For I know, I shall mope for days on end, when you do that to one of your own. Your loving daughter you raised with so much love and affection. This affliction hits you, now. It tears me from within. It tears me apart, dear father. Lump in my throat, you are not around to mend.

I think of you and my mother. How beautiful she looks? Her skin, fair, soft in the moonlight glow, midnight of cascading hair. You sitting by her side, holding each other in the clear, dazzling light, propped up by stars of a night; listening to Andrea Bocelli, singing, reciting Tagore and Nazrul Islam's poetry. Tonight, you're a different person, sensitive, caring, and romantic, playing chess, laughing at silly, odd jokes, talking vibrantly, and being the perceptive mind that you are.

Bocelli's voice was smooth like an aluminium sheet over a placid sea. The blind seer, who saw how he could conquer; his vision peerless in his understanding of the world. But father, your mind, to the contrary, was not, hence your visions blurry. Dear Father, did you not see it coming?

Alas! You just called my mother, your mother. Mother knows not that one day, you'll not remember the distant past, and forget the formidable immediate. Mother knows not until this day, that you would be looking at the world through your netted mind. You, who made so many sacrifices, once. Your charities saved lives. Your readings, misgivings, your writings, musings, your first-class brain, a full life.

Who now holds Shakespeare's complete works in his hands and pretends to read it. You, who knows enough to hold the book, although the words may fall through the holes of your once whole brain. Words melt away, Words writ in water. But you did that much, at least. Hold the book closely enough, salient like salinity to an ocean, faithful to your art; hold your pen upright, to your diary. I often watched you, a little girl in awe, how you cut and pasted sentences with scissors, in those days, without computers. How you edited; you knew your words so well, in your meaningful hay day.

You took me to see a circus once. You caged me within your arms, dear father, so no one would brush past me, or hurt me inadvertently in the crowd-filled circus park. I have not forgotten anything, Father. But you have. Your memory has lapsed. You go out for random walks, beyond the rail tracks, and forget your home, the little blue house. These long walks back, not wilfully wayward, but to ensure safety, I had to lock you in the house, so you would not lose your way, back to us.

Your brilliant mind, the much-lauded works, and the published newspaper pieces bear testimony to that. Now, you forget people's names, friend's names, your children's names. Oh! Forget-me-not, dear father. I cannot endure this. But if it's in your genes, then you cannot help it. How helpless people are when they cannot remember, or forget the next word. How overwhelmingly, helpless it must be, when you can't even recognise your beloved wife, let alone the names of great writers of all times, Iris Murdoch. Today you have shared the same fate. Iris Murdoch, who knew so much, then knew not what words to put in a sentence string.

What sort of morbidity is this within your mind? How do you interpret when you see faces? This blinding world of nothingness, yet, nearly, not half as blind as the world of Andrea Bocelli of notes, rhythm, tunes, and modulation. Every chord, he feels. Every spice on his palate explodes in a celebration of this world, which has thus far distanced itself from you, and rendered it off-limits, that you descend

120

into this chaotic place of the discordant beat of no taste, certainly no musical vibrations. In severe cold, you forget to put your black coat on. And you forget to select shoes from your wardrobe of hundred-pair collections.

You decline sharply, to a merciless, dull spot of muteness. Living in this speechless world is perhaps much braver than we're willing to give it credit. Out of bare ignorance, it must feel like a black hole, which no light can ever penetrate. This life of forgetfulness, forgetting, and to forget, at a frightening pace. All things, present, near past, and then distant past, information lost in this fretful deep well, things, names, places, and babbles.

Forget-me-not, dear Father. For I'm your loving daughter, who may one day follow in your footsteps, like many demented others. How rapidly this disease grows, accelerates to invade the most private thoughts and not so private. The most cherished ideals, blighted in the brain, just as vices of every deplorable sin, leaving no room for confessions, amendments, let alone forgiveness. To become a blank slate, a vacuum without any traces of vices, or virtues, records of ever praying at evensong. A flat line, father, is all you display, a mere shadow of yourself without smiles, breathing expressionless and wordless, statued on the sofa or lying stiff on the bed. Mother by your side, as ever; we are around, but a faceless number to you. Your books and your writing desk stare at you, dear Father. Even the inanimate speaks volumes.

Why though, father dear, my sorrows, vapid, unbound. I miss you. I miss you. I get claustrophobic, thinking of you. I know not "How do you feel in your mind, the claustrophobia of a kind?" Indescribable that you will never be able to express. No more, no less, it is you though, who ultimately carries the burden of wealth in that paradoxical net of your brain, knitting this wealth of knowledge of all the lights, the world cannot see. Nor reach new heights. Knowledge of this ugly barred condition eludes wisdom and sanity, the world waits to garner more brains as much brawn.

First published by *The Cabinet of Heed*, issue 26, Ireland, November 2019

Turin Fog

The rain dripped: drip, drip, drip. The sound distracted me from watching a movie on Netflix, Tinker Sailor Soldier Spy, lying on the sofa, with my socked feet dangling over an armrest. My partner and I, engaged in intermittent chats about moles in the murky world of espionage, and betrayal, the dark evening's rain.

"Who do you think is the mole?" he asked.

"Hard to tell, really," I responded. "The narrative is too convoluted. Le Carré is one of those few writers who know how to create atmospheric novels, drawing them out of a stream-of-consciousness mind for perfect cinematic effect."

"This movie has nothing to do with stream-of-consciousness.

"Not, a stream-of-consciousness? What would you call this continuous switch between distant past, and present then?"

"A hard narrative, but not that," he declared.

"Oh! You can be so stubborn."

A veil of silence fell in the room, like a graveyard shift. The movie grabbed all our attention, to the effect that we pretended to be like perfect strangers in a theatre, sitting in a hall, not communicating. We couldn't anymore, not without descending to vulgar disagreements. The rains lashed straight through my mind. The dark space between us, and the dreary world of the movies, seemed aligned, existing in a parallel string world.

Time is of the essence, the backward and the forward motion of the narrative. Back in time, it had rained another night like this. I sat on a bench in an alley in Turin, holding an umbrella upright, under a sallow street lamp post. Someone bumped into me. I, a Russian spy. This stranger looked at my eyes, and I invited him under my umbrella. We walked towards a café. That was our den. But the man didn't know that I was a spy. We shared my bed upstairs. At midnight, he said, he wanted to leave.

"Go? The night isn't even over, yet?" I asked.

"Ah! My love, I still must go," he answered.

"But why? We're just getting started."

"Are we?" he asked.

"Aren't we?" I asked. "What?"

His stun gun silenced me. But I wasn't quite dead, yet. I saw him disappear in the rain fog. Tinker Tailor Soldier Spy, had also come to an end. The mole got killed, but the story in my head hadn't quite finished. The man who stunned me walked away into the rain. I realise that he was a spy too. He had his orders to kill me. But he stunned me instead. As he walked in the rain, without an umbrella, he decided to stand under shelter. Another man passed by and handed him a parcel. He opened it. There were some instructions. There was a plane ticket for Budapest. He waited for the rain to abate. At this hour, there were no taxis. It was a long walk to his hotel. He entered and into his room. As soon as he closed the door, he knew he wasn't alone. Someone in the room turned around and he saw me. He wasn't startled but smiled. I smiled too.

"That stun worked," I said.

He said, "Well you need a make-over, now. Because I confirmed with my agency that you were dead. They've given me another assignment for Budapest, now."

My partner turned off the TV. This spy who came in the rain didn't kill me. Because he was my Russian colleague. He knew I was a mole, leaking information to the enemy. He did the same. All part of the game. The Russians wanted me dead, but didn't know he too was a double agent.

I cut my hair short and coloured it black in the hotel bathroom. I put a Turkish dress on and a headscarf to cover my hair. Then we went out of the hotel and on our way to Hungary. There was an assembly of world leaders. He sent me to assassinate the Russian, representative.

"To kill a Russian?" I asked.

"Yes, only then can we defect to the USA. You're dead to the Russians, anyway. They'll never suspect you."

In Budapest, I stood by a window and had the target in the crosshairs. This was a meeting on gun-ban. A shot came out of my gun. The target fell. But, I was hit too. Who leaked this? Why? I saw the killer. It was him.

I was seeing crows in the Budapest summer's skies. After that, I blacked out.

First published by *Sage Cigarettes*. Yule Issue Special Edition, USA, 2019

Perforation

My time was up. The clock had stopped. My stilly pupils stared. Cold. My body fell like Filbert. Stiff. It occurred at the stroke of midnight when the hours froze. I rose to a height, and saw my inert body, once conscious and full of lights, had now been sucked out of all its virtuous nuances and delights.

A boat waited on the River Erebos, on the western edge of the mortal world. A hooded boatman stood with an oar. I looked at him and winked to say I wasn't quite done yet. I looked down at my body, which had now been removed and lowered six feet below. But my good friends thought I must still feel the thirst. For I saw them place cups of water in the room where I had once been. To not disappoint them, I stooped to the ground and sipped the water wholly swooping drown.

"Do spirits drink water?" I heard my friend ask her companion.

"Apparently, yes, look at the level of water in that cup. It has halved in twenty-four hours."

"True, and true it is, that's a visible reality."

They continued to place brimming cups of water on the table in that room for me. There was a perforation. I entered this world, which was mine just an hour ago. And I continued to drink it every day, as the sage boatman reminded me that we must be on our way. But I refused to hearken to his words of wisdom, for I saw how my friends grieved down there for me.

"Do they even realise what happened here?"

I asked the boatman who nodded his hooded, blackhead in the dark and said, "They know, but not enough to know the magic that you are. They know nothing of the bigger magic that you're to be united soon.

"But I have been banished from my home, my body," I cried.

"You're the soul, the magic that propelled consciousness in that melting body that they do not know."

"This world, *A Midsummer's Night's Dream*, conjured by the potion of Puck's magic, no?" I ask the boatman.

"It is a sentient potion, which you're a small fraction of," he replied.

"Look, look at them, how puzzled they look, because I, now the unseen, had drunk the water which they lovingly put aside every day for me."

"Ah, but, but you're a mist leaked out of the sullied body; you lay outside of the bottle. You must come with me at once, not enter a bodily world you do not exist in any longer."

But I still hadn't stepped into the boat yet. My once magical body, now starved of it, was composting.

Who was I? What was I? I have drunk from the topped cup, and halved the water down, to trick them into believing that the full-bodied life was a reality. Or like a band-aid to a wound, I had drunk from a cup of solace for my aggrieved friends to make them believe that in death I was living. But I was – who I was – much larger than life or this sprite; I was a part of that mystifying magic of nuanced lights, not just the energy potions packed into this leaking body which appeared to be, I. The boatman was right. I must go. Half-cup lures must cease to chase a fuller consciousness of the deceased; being a part of which was the real, I. That was my home far beyond.

First published by *Impspired Magazine*, Issue 12 online/Volume Six, UK, 2021

Sonorous Wave

Two helicopters flew over our heads, like a duo dragonfly in the autumn sky. This afternoon, my sister and I sat under an old oak tree in our garden by the River Bhairab. Those were the days when we chatted silly and talked about every nonsense that entered our heads, giggling over nothing.

"You always live in your head," my sister declared.

"Let me guess, you don't like that. This life of the mind kind o' thing," I laughed.

"You know how it is, thinking, dreaming." I laughed first, then she laughed with me.

I hadn't actually realised it, until now that she mentioned it. Yes, I was the more reflective one, she, the extroverted. But that was all the difference we had; we both stood on a common ground of compassion. Well-bonded in togetherness.

When we were growing up, many of the political discussions in our house centred around the partition of India. Discussions which shaped our world views, so much so that they made us opinionated. We always heard about these eternal qualms between the Hindus and the Muslims. The Hindus suffered in the hands of Muslims during partition, and now it was the Muslims' turn to suffer in the hands of the Hindus. The power shifts, after the British had left. The crooked history never left us at peace, not today, not ever; if any, it made us even more crooked, hating everyone, in our loveless lives. These clockwise and anticlockwise motions of emotions ran hot and cold, politics played and churned out generations of despicable events.

Dramas that we saw around our kitchen table bore that testament. Our parents endlessly bickered over what should

128

have been the right course. Disagreements led to high levels of anger, at times, shouts grew louder, and arguments deepened. We listened and left the table when we couldn't endure it anymore. We started living a distorted reality of ideas.

I looked up at the sky, such a serene afternoon, today. At the far end of the garden, our gardener weeded netted locks from a thorny rose tree. He looked at us and nodded a greeting with a smile. We smiled back. The garden looked deliciously luxuriant or decadent, this time of the year. It burst into all sorts of nature's vibrancy, as the colours of spring changed to warm scarlet, deep magenta, sea turtle emerald, and saffron pouring onto our lawn. Impeccable was the word that summed it up. However, the gardener's intrepid work at cleaning the fallen, decrepit leaves, could not be ignored. It was his job to bring the garden to a full bloom every spring, of roses, white jasmine, and pink daisies, and his job as well to clean it all up throughout autumn. Yes, pink daisies, the most prolific of all, the Nordic goddess, Freya's sacred colour, symbolising love, beauty, and fertility.

The gardener couldn't do much to change the seasons' natural laws. In autumn and in winter, the colours faded anyway. However, it all became replenished and resplendent, the next monsoon, when all the colours returned. He cared for the garden. It showed, how tirelessly, he kept at it, sprucing it up from fertilising every priceless tree to watering them diligently. He never slept or ate. He lived over by the river, in this hut, with a leaky roof, through which rainwater dropped. But, he seemed to enjoy this drip and didn't bother to fix it.

"It is beautiful, wouldn't you agree?" I asked my sister.

She looked at the garden, then at the gardener, and then his broken hut by the river. And nodded in agreement.

"Do you think he is in love?" she asked.

"Maybe, we never really speak to him, do we?" I said.

"Hmm. I wonder sometimes."

"We do speculate a lot," I laughed.

She laughed with me. The gardener overheard. The tinkle and the words carried over by the autumnal air.

"Should we ask him?" asked my feisty sister.

"About what? If he is in love?" I asked in disbelief.

"Yes, if he can create this lush place of such breathing, blooming flowers, he must have a heart, too; sensitive enough to love and to kiss." The gardener, in my thoughts, swam in the deep river, and then suddenly, he kissed a girl there, in the river's depth, a secret he harboured. He somersaulted in the water and swam away.

I looked at her puzzled. "You do realise, our parents would kill us if they heard us speak of gardener's love life."

"Yes, I do realise. Do you think life would be any less miserable with gardener than it is right now? To the contrary, life may flourish."

They both looked at his hut. And thought about how the rainwater never affected him. Then there was a cry. It came from the gardener. We rushed towards him. He cut off his index finger and then tried to re-attach it. Red blood oozed out on the manicured lawn. A snake had bitten him, a brown, poisonous viper. It slithered away right before us.

"Oh! No!" we screamed. "You must go to surgery at once.

"It's okay. I'll go to my hut and rest. I'll be fine tomorrow."

"But you've lost so much blood."

We couldn't tell if he heard us. He dropped the finger and walked away. My sister began to run, but towards the kitchen to ask the chef if he could make some broth for the gardener. In a bit, she returned with a bowl of broth, while I hung around the garden, and saw how the soil soaked all his blood; the blue finger lay inert. She returned with the broth. We went to the hut. The hut was bare as bones. We heard the sonorous river convey the following:

Roof's torn portal led to spacetime above;
Earthlings seen as copious, but tiny pebbles on the top;
Gardener's elusive, ubiquitous apparition, to summon;
Holler life's tales of bittersweet paradox.

First published by *The Cabinet of Heed* Issue 27, Ireland, December 2019

Same Page

I saw my friend in my bedroom.

He said, "I'm leaving."

"Aren't you supposed to be in the hospital? Why are you in my bedroom at midnight?"

Like a spectre, he disappeared. I tried to get some sleep after that. But I kept on thinking of his illuminated shape in the dark. He looked perfectly healthy, and he smiled like a man of thirty. He was like this dream I had once about my father who had passed away some years now. It was a very strange dream.

I had dreamt that I was trying to lock these two sliding, security doors, but I couldn't. I gave up and walked back. I sat down on a sofa in the well-lit living room. Just when I saw them, they stood outside the two doors. A coal tar of dark night splattered across space. The two men were standing here. At the entrance of one door my father stood. He had two suitcases with him. He smiled and waited for my invitation to enter. He put his two suitcases down by his side on the ground. Too excited to see him, I smiled back. I rose from the sofa, to greet him. Just when I saw the other. This one was a stranger. Perhaps my father's companion. He also stood with his two suitcases at the door. His smiles were not as cordial as my father's. They were playful and tentative, and hovered on his lips. My father looked stalky and slender in his long white shirt and white trousers. His companion, short and chubby. He wore an off white shirt and long pants.

My father looked full-blooded, tight and fit, a young man in his early thirties; the stranger, also in his youth. Had they come over to visit me? Perhaps, he and his companions were passing through; they dropped by. They wanted to come in. But I didn't invite them in. I stood resolutely rooted to the ground in the middle of the bright room, waiting to see what happened next. They waited, out in the dark, if I offered them food and drink. They must have been knackered with exhaustion. They needed a rest. But I didn't offer them any. I didn't move; neither did they. They kept smiling and looking at me, two suitcases by the side. Were they time travelling? Why? He looked exactly my age. My father was a citizen of a parallel universe. He had to be. Same with the companion; they may have accidentally slipped through a netted time rip. I felt ashamed of my behaviour that I didn't invite them. They teetered on the brink of seamless fantasy and reality. Yes, my father was in my space. He looked exactly the same age as me. The doors were open, but they didn't force entry. Because they had become outsiders.

The next morning, I decided to pay a visit to my friend at the hospital. There was a strong wind. It whistled a dirge, as it swept the dry leaves of spring. I walked against the gust to get there. I had to find out that he was okay. In the hospital building, I walked towards his cabin; I had the strangest premonition. What if he actually was in my room, last night? As I came closer to his room, I saw him in bed from a distance. He had just turned over on his bed, facing me. He smiled as though he expected me. I lifted my arm and waved. He kept on looking at me in a really strange way. When I was finally at his bedside, he tried to sit. I helped him.

"Well, how are you?"
"I'm back in my bed now, That's a relief."
"What do you mean?" I asked.
"I saw my own body sleeping in this bed, last night."
"Really? How is that possible?"

133

"Believe it or not, I was up there, hanging by the ceiling. I saw my whole life from there. It was as though I was on a fast-moving train. And through the carriage window, I could see myself, crawling, walking, schooling and now sleeping in this bed."

"Now that is very strange. Because, I saw you too, in my bedroom last night. You looked healthy, youthful, full of life."

"You did?"

"Yes, I did."

"On that train, I also saw you, playing as children, getting old, decrepit. Life went so fast, in a flash."

"I don't really know what happened. Were you hallucinating?" I asked.

"The nurses said so. And then at one stage, I saw the white light, beckoning me to follow it."

"What happened after that?"

"I nearly went after it. But the next moment, I was awake. Right here in bed. I saw nurses and doctors pouring over me. They told me I was clinically dead for a few minutes."

"Clinically dead? What does that even mean? Either one is dead or not dead."

"It means that I'd died for a few minutes."

"Your soul or chemistry, whatever it is, was outside this vessel, that we call a body," I said.

He nodded. And then the penny dropped for me. Human consciousness could survive outside the body and roam freely. Last night, an episode had occurred in the hospital, in this very room, but I saw him in my bedroom, a long way away from the hospital.

"What now?" I asked.

"Let's go for a walk," he suggested.

"In this gusty wind?"

We both looked out through the hospital window. Wavering winds blew in a clear blue sky. The nurses in white walked through the corridors. White walls.

"We're still here." I winked.

"It's time," he replied.

First published by *Sage Cigarettes*, Yule Issue Special Edition, USA, December 2019

A Blinding Flash

Just when Lizzy Crimson was leaving the art exhibition, a black and white picture hanging on the far side of a wall caught her attention. It was unbelievably mesmerising, and surrealistic. It looked like a downing of the sun at night. But the bright light that it emanated was white and diffused. The black patches were like ash clouds. Strands of tree branches swayed across the portrait.

Lizzy was drawn like a magnet to iron ore. She hadn't seen anything like it. She stood before it and gazed. Seconds and minutes passed, she couldn't figure it out. Then an odd hour passed, and still, she didn't know what she was looking at. At a glimpse, the image didn't make much sense. It looked like the clouds of night. The round sun is going down. But this could not be because there wouldn't be the sun at night. Could the round ball be a full moon then? That was plausible, however, the twigs looked far too thin for any branch of a tree.

Anything could be possible in surrealism, she knew. But she wasn't convinced. She looked deeper and deeper. She didn't read the note pinned by the picture, because she was so enamoured by the rawness of the quality of the art. Then when she wasn't happy with any of her interpretations, she sat down in front of it feeling miffed. She tried to see it from a different perspective. And from this angle, she saw something. A sensation ran through her. She saw something different. It was neither the sun, nor the moon, or the stark pointy branches sticking out like skeletal fingers. It was the other. The otherness that shook her.

She took a closer look, even closer. Now she made a breakthrough. The image was not surrealistic, but hyper-realistic. It was a scanned image. A scan of the human eye in the back of one's head. The twigs were but thin wisps of hair falling across the scanning camera.

"By Jove, I would never have known that the scan of the back of the eye could look so beautifully nature-like in black and white," she mused. "But then the beautiful band of a colourful rainbow didn't look like the rainbow we viewed either in hyper-reality. It looked different, a collection of water droplets, of different sizes and shapes. The two distinct worlds of the same reality existed simultaneously; one hinging on the other in perfect harmony."

First published by *Academy of the Heart and Mind*, USA, April 2020

Dolly

"Not without her," Ana screamed. "I'm not leaving without Doll."

But the police officer kept pestering. She put Ana in handcuffs. Ana yelled at the constable. She pleaded. But the resolute officer didn't budge. She told Ana that she must leave without her doll. For it was she, who was in trouble, not her doll. Ana realised that the police officer didn't understand that Dolly was her security blanket, and now always. Ever since she was five, now fifteen.

"Trouble?" she screamed. "You say, I'm in trouble? A parasite under the radar until you caught me out?"

"What else would you call yourselves? You, downy mildew of festering? You steal buns from that bakery there."

"I only steal for hunger."

"Little Snitch! I'll get you sorted out."

"Ha! I have been like this since I was five. I sold flowers on Harlon Street, an orphan, and a phantom to most. Those who saw my flowers never saw me; I was invisible to them, camouflaged like a screech owl on a living bark. Then one day, someone noticed me," she said.

"Who? Who noticed you?" asked the police constable.

"He did. The big man. One evening, it rained. I appeared at his car window with a bunch of yellow chrysanthemums. He rolled down his windows and offered me money. He told me to take the money and re-sell the wet bunch. Just when the lights changed, I dropped the flowers on his lap, saying that he must take them or else Dolly may get offended. The man drove away.

She looked down at the grooved pavement littered with torn plastic bags. A bed made out of slippery bags for a slippery life.

"Is this any way to live? You should be ashamed of your life?" The constable yelled.

"Yeah? Do you have a better idea? Where were you, when they took me? I had almost become the big men's playing doll. Where were you when those leeches nearly lay me down in their valley, the night's under-bridge?"

Another rain began as Ana told her story, how the same car came back the next night, and she, a mere child of ten ran towards it to sell some more. But this time, the driver opened the car door, instead of a window. He tried to entice her with bundles of money. The girl was frightened and ran away that night.

The end of her flower-selling days came the next evening. This time she had Dolly with her. That car was on the street. She stood squeezed in between the traffic jam. Two strong hands grabbed her and pulled her inside.

She fretted, twisted, and turned. Ana fell asleep gripping Dolly close to her chest. The car sped along; they reached a mansion. The heavy doors opened, and a woman appeared. She came to the car and took Ana inside. They entered a pink bedroom. She scoffed at her, "Not another word." Weeks and months passed. She was kept all to herself in this pink bedroom. It was full of dolls. The woman dolled her up too, with beautiful dresses, and new make-up. But she missed her street.

Then one day, the man summoned her into the living room she hadn't seen in many days. But he wasn't alone. He was with others.

"What's your name, little girl?" asked another man.

She replied, shyly, "Ana,"

"Lovely name, Ana. Go pack a small bag, I want to take you out."

A cold shiver ran through her. She was going out with this strange man. Maybe, this could open up an escape route. In her room, she packed a pink suitcase and picked up Dolly. She came back into the living room. The man took her hand and walked her out of the palace. Ana never saw this palace again, the woman, or the first man. They climbed into another car that the new man drove. In the car, he looked at her and slid his hand under Ana's skirt. Ana felt odd. She tried to move away from him. By now he had started his car, and the car sped down a highway.

"Where are you taking me?" Ana asked.

"You'll see. Don't be afraid."

Ana began to cry. She screamed so much that the man had to stop his car. He took Ana by her shoulders and shook them.

"Stop this. Stop this at once. Or else I'll kill you."

Ana cowed before his rage. He glowered at her and restarted his car. She looked at her doll and pressed her close to her chest. Her nails dug deep into the doll's cascading hair. She thought of her flowers, the delicate white, yellow, pink chrysanthemum petals. How they bloomed before her and perished. Her freedom on the street, her kind boss, the owner of the flower shop. Some days, she got paid, some days, she didn't. Some days she ate, some days she didn't. It all depended on the sale. But this? Anything was better than this. She fought her miserable thoughts. This new place, she didn't know. Where was she going to go? The driver stopped the car, yet again. He got out, locking her inside. Ana's restive mind thought of a way out. She held her Dolly tight and said.

"Dear Dolly, I will take you out of here. I won't let that bastard touch you."

The doll looked at her and blinked. She had wings. She rose from her lap like a dot of light. There was a sound of the window locks clicking and popping straight up. The car doors flung open. Bright lights in her eyes, Dolly smiled. Ana was free. She jumped out of the car. She fled. She fled with Dolly and never looked back. The man had gone to buy coffee, she imagined. She pictured him back into the car, looking frantically for Ana. But all he found was her pink suitcase, perched neatly up against the seat's leather base.

First published in *Transformations*, winning entries for the 2020 Waterloo Festival Writing Competition, UK, 2020

Bengal, 1971

It was lunchtime in Madhupur. Taramon, a motherless farmer's daughter of twenty-four, was just getting ready to sit down with her four siblings for lunch. Their father had left for the field early in the morning. The farmer didn't join them for lunch. A mat had been rolled out on the mud floor. Taramon brought out the food in three small bowls of rice, daal, and curried fish. Stooping over, she put them down on the mat. The cuckoo bird's intermittent whistles in the breezy, bamboo bush serenaded this heavy afternoon of quietness.

Then, the sounds came. Oh! It was awful. Sounds blasted through the skies. A gunshot. A gunshot which shook them to the core. Birds took off in anxious flights, wings like inverted flying buttresses. They hadn't even sat down on the mat when a boy ran into the front yard. Taramon knew him. He was the neighbour's son, Shuvo. She shot a glance at him and asked, "What's this sound?"
Her question perplexed him.
"Don't you know?"
"Know what?"
"That the enemy is here?"
The enemy? Already?"
"Yes, already! And people are fleeing like crazy," he said.
"Why are you still here then?"
"I was in the field when I saw a gunboat up the river. I ran. I ran as fast as I could; I ran home to my parents. They were gone by then."
"Gone? Where to?"
"I don't know."
The boy broke down in tears. Taramon didn't wait. She

142

rushed out of the hut. Shuvo and her siblings followed her right behind. They ran through the tranquil bush by their mud hut. On the way, they found others, their hapless friends, Shuvo's parents, and her father in a frenzy. Some carried crying babies. Others carried elderly parents, but racing towards the Indian border. In the midst, one young mother turned around and began to push her way back to the village. Taramon stood in her way. The mother looked at Taramon and tried to get past her howling, like the wild monsoon winds over the swollen, serpentine river.

"Don't," she said. "Don't. My, my baby. She was asleep. I had to leave her by herself to go to work. She, in the house. I was in the field when they chased me out. I panicked. Oh! I left her in the house. She sleeps, my baby. My baby will now burn to a cinder."

Taramon would not let her go. She embraced the mother tight and turned her around. Others helped Taramon guide her back into the panic-stricken procession. The woman was petrified. She looked at nothing. Silent, like a broken clock that had stopped ticking. A black smoke rose over the horizon. A crimson sky loomed.

_____

First published by *FlashBack Fiction, UK, 2020*

Pink Toenails

Then the mountains spoke. Voiced it in chorus, on the ancient land of Turag. A world where trees walked, winds cried, rivers sang and the mountains talked. This place, is not for humans to reside anymore, but for natural lives and artificial intelligence. Turag, yes, this place, because humans have long been obliterated, like dinosaurs before them. Since then robots have replaced them. The organic world even as we speak, ceased to exist, as autumnal dirge swept through the pine forests of dead wood.

They all witnessed it: the sky, the oceans, and the mountains. But their voices couldn't be heard. In the days of humans, everyone thought they were mute, who neither heard nor spoke. But humans were wrong. They communicated and witnessed every human history. Humans didn't see what they saw. Just as well, they saw the end of the world. They saw it all coming. There was too much clunky background noise. Humans were a noisy lot.

Turag, once a lush plateau. Birds frolicked in the rain. Wheat and rice grass grew and wavered under an autumn sky. Children played around, while mothers bar-b-qued corn over open fire-pits. Smoke nearly choked the neighbouring mountains of the plateau. But the mountains never complained. They smiled and took it all in their stride. They waited patiently for a miracle to happen.

In the meantime, billions of years of civilisation passed. Generations toppled one another. Kings died to make way for the new. Power corrupted Kings. Mighty Kings they might have been, who won battles, and killed people on the mountain steppes. The green fields turned scarlet, replacing the many resplendent shades. But wins and expansions were all that mattered to the Kings, one more despotic than the other, often sacrificed the innocent for self-aggrandisement, and cared not much at all for justice, whether or not justice was meted out. Then a time came when nature revolted. Fields stopped producing bumper crops. Rains decided not to dole out the bountiful properties of the rainbow. Leaves shrivelled up. Darkness blighted the sun. Blood moon lit the world. Machines were empowered. This new age of machines initiated a different kind of rage. An annihilation of the humans was underway, to take possession of the land. They didn't need nature to feed them, and neither did they care to find beauty in it. Humans, long gone.

"Could men not have predicted this?" asked the blood moon to the mountains.

"They could very well have because they were the ones to make these machines. But men ignored it in a haste to chase success," the mountains answered. The veiled sun conceded. The mountains said. "Enter our caves and view the paintings there; stories of life foreshadowed on the dim walls. But men paid no heed. Too much background noise; they came from war drums, drunken cheers of vacuous victories, and wonton amusements. Noises shrouded men's judgment for everything that came to pass. Fools, they were fools! Those men, whose wisdom failed them. Only the stars knew how reckless they were. The massive destruction of innocent lives. Timeless settlements and resettlements, of nearly broken bones and spirits of men, women, and children. They looked like scattered peas to the gods above. Still, men endeavoured to build communities and strange dwellings to shield themselves from showers, storms, and blustery winds. They chose to ignore the transience of life. They stopped to think that the life-giving, precious air, their lifeline, was sourced from an outer world; that they had no control over. The last breath taken, very well could be on those battlefields. Relentless battles, as if there were no tomorrows. Mortals inhaled this infinite air to harness what little strengths they could and stored them within their caged shells. A mortal existence, without any rhyme or reason. The immortals while they remained, so tied humans to timelines, and made them mortals. Ah! But humans didn't think that far ahead. Too limited for predictions. That their passions exultant, looped them up into this paradox. This paradox would also lead to the destruction of the human race. "By far, their intelligence caused this downfall," said Blood-moon. "Did they have a choice?"

"Well, you and I seemed to have outlived humans."

While they had this conversation, a dust storm picked up on the far side of the plateau. A russet gust of winds rolled in and darkened the mountains, clogged up its crevices and valleys. It covered the blood-moon too, rendering a sad world to further gloom. This wasn't the end surely? The mountains thought. They had difficulty breathing; the air had ceased. The trees stopped walking to get their bearings back; the rivers stopped singing. They broke out into hiccups and coughs. These tumults in the surroundings, shook the peace. No human hand at play, to create this havoc. The machines ran amok, and kept losing their vital parts. There was no one to fix them. Machines could doctor one another, but they didn't get that opportunity. Because, even they couldn't predict this. A human failing of flawed design, to be certain.

An impending disaster loomed. Another kind of warfare started within nature itself. The winds clashed with the rising tide. Mountains stood guard, to stop the storm from going any further. But the lightning then befell the mountain tips. Series of volcanic eruptions, and melted glaciers paved the way to pandemonium. The overflowed lava wedded the falling lightnings, and danced in spiralled tango. Complete chaos beset the land of Turag. In the wake of a present danger, the blood-moon shot out of sight. The storms, the lightning, left history in awe. Then a heat wave surged. Turag was hot again. Turag hotting up! The lava ran in a rivulet towards the swelling seas. The oceans submerged the mountains. The plateau of Turag, now under water, saw another breathing world beneath the oceans. Once again there was life. Mermaids swam unhindered. A clear sun ruled and gave humans a second chance.

First published by *Metachrosis Literary Magazine*, Dundee University, Scotland, 2023

Blue, Grey, and Lavender

Grass had become dehydrated. Trees poured out saffron. Brittle straws clung to Mother Earth, a stream of orange lawn. The soil was made of sand. It caved in and became hollow land. A bowl for my soul where I hid like a mole. I felt nothing at first. Then a hunger rose. I ate my hunger, I walked in a dream. Dream of life. There was silence in my heart. It whispered an autumnal dirge. On the outpost of a war, a fallen soldier noted lights of nuanced whites and many ugly plights.

Then I stood before a ship. This was but a spectre of a ship, full of passengers on board. They held a globed sceptre, and goblets which lacked lustre; drunken spectators, smiley faces of lime plasters. They were flying apparitions of greater imaginations, once Kings and Queens, in powerful human bodies. They were here, fighting like crazy for the love of the land, now pushed up daisies. I waited out on the shore, as the ship slowly anchored. Deep into the blues of an oceanic wonder, I watched to catch the Kings' flounder. They rose from their seats and somersaulted, for they'd become sprites of glowing gases.

I wondered why they looked like this. Also, the phantom ship, a vessel of uncovered ribs. Why did they drink and eat indeed? Then I realised, it was just a flash of the worldly pleasures, unabashedly brash. The clinging of my flesh under the skinned mesh, I'd passed into the sublime and couldn't care less; briefly without a cure, my mind wasn't too sure. But I could breathe spots of fresh air, in this warfare, except there were no cries, only stilly stares. The bullets were gone, and the soldiers slept in peace, in their little crypts. Some had shut eyelids, others in half-open slits.

In a daze, this fuzzy maze, was I caught up in another war craze? The dances of the lights led me on, but I felt like a dunce myself in tattered clothes and all. Because, I was still wearing a soldier's uniform, but pretty sure I didn't need one. Then I felt a rush of adrenaline. I was at the boundary lane until I heard a call from my mom at dawn. She'd come into my room, a patched blanket hot off the loom; she was no loon, neither a shadow of doom.

"Wake up, wake up, you fool," she then crooned.

First published by *Setu Bilingual Journal Flash Fiction Section*, India, May 2020

faUx paS

There was banter at the dinner table. People laughed at somebody's jest. These boisterous gestures of joy distracted me. There were at least twenty people seated here, and the clamour of cutlery and talks rose to high-pitched peals. Then the butler entered with a tray in his beefy hands. On the tray, I saw many bowls of the pewter brand. He placed them in front of each person. Most people knew what to do with them. I only had a foray of inkling. I looked away from everyone. I looked at the bowl before me. It held some water and a slice of lemon. I picked up the bowl in my hands and slowly brought it up to my lips. Between my lips, I placed the pewter rim and drank the water straight off its brim. Dead silence dropped in the room. People who didn't even steal a glance until now inclined their heads all towards me. I wasn't sure what I had done to become the centre of this sudden attention. My perplexity compounded when I saw what they did. Finger bowl it was. A mistake made by me. They did just what they were meant to do: dip their nimble fingers into them, and rub them elegantly. I looked at my fingers and deemed them to be clean.

I noted that my hostess, Nancy, and Mark suppressed a smile. There was nothing I could do now or anyone else for that matter. No amount of cover-ups could hide what I had done. Oh! I wanted to cut those fingers off. Pull out the nails. That they were meant to be in the anointed water of the holy grail. I felt like running away. But I couldn't do that either. I couldn't make an egress, because something had pinned me to the chair. Dried butterflies encased in collector's possession, I just sat glumly like a frog on a lily pad, in the wake of a rain. Yes, I sat, sat through it, while they watched me in shock and horror and ridiculed me. Inwardly they said, I wasn't sophisticated. I didn't know the decorum of the kingdom. I knew exactly, every odd thought that crossed their heads. An anomaly had occurred, an oddity took place, right before their eyes, at this dinner table tonight. As much as I fancied not to appear crude, the brute in everyone, the jury was still out. I knew what they thought, but I didn't know what they would do to me. I, still sitting, becoming, and gradually coming to my senses that the socialites would perhaps abandon me, and kick me out. How dare I brush shoulders with the creams and the gleams of these bunch of elites. While they wondered what to do with me, I thought of a ruse. I decided enough was enough, I was going to save myself from this humiliation at any cost. I wanted to normalise. I still wanted to be in. I allowed some fleeting seconds of these petrified moments. Then I stood up on my two heels. I pushed my chair back hard; it fell resoundingly on the floor, to their surprise. I walked up two steps to the door and asked a man standing here, to fetch me a pen and sheets of white paper.

While my audience floundered, I waited for my ammunition. The pen and the papers arrived, and I took them in my stride. I quickly laid out sheets of paper on the floor and etched a few parallels and disjointed poles. I connected the dots and sketched a tall picture of its opulence, not to mention the ambiance. It was a sketch of this dinner table, and everyone was seated there with calm demeanours. The frozen, confused expressions and detailed images, replete with lavish foods, this festive occasion. The pewter bowls were there too, the cause of the faux pas.

When my sketching was complete, I held it up in the lights. The disbelief in their eyes said it all. That I could paint a picture of this magnitude. Some lauded, and others screamed out, "Say, did you do that on purpose, so you could catch the moment on canvas?" I took this opportunity and bowed low to ask for forgiveness and to tell purportedly, "that it was indeed the intent all along." The crowd cheered, they clapped and forgot about this splendid faux pas. I titled the painting, faUx paS, and then gifted it to my host. This painting received a prestigious award. Another version survived in the Gallery of Modern Arts. However, It was never for sale, because it was the painting which had saved my soul, a re-entry ticket into the world unknown.

It wasn't the elites that I feared, but my defeat. I wouldn't consider a feat. My painting may have saved me from one faux pas; still, many may await in the future repository. After all, it was the few odd faux pas that sent the Boleyn sister off to the gallows to her beheaded misery. The one who spoke her mind, her tongue a shaper bind; in a less forgiving world, faux pas could cause enormous abuse. Transforming Henry's love into fatal discontent, surely, her faux pas were made at countless social events.

People didn't know the environment that bred them. Atonements may follow, and friendships may mend, to define "Cleopatra as not a pretty woman". Or refer to Wales as "part of England"; regardless, history will not relent. And neither would records bend, just because faux pas are an embarrassment.

First published by *Straylight Literary Magazine*, USA, March 2020

Rain and Coffee

As lightning crackled, Claudia drew the curtains apart. She stood before the long French windows of her penthouse apartment and looked down at a wet alley. The cobblestones of the boulevard shone in the rain falling from dismal clouds. It hadn't rained for days. She yawned and then she stretched. Across the boulevard, a boulangerie just opened for the day. She saw a young baker bringing out a basket of fresh croissants. He displayed them in a glassed cove. They were enticing, particularly today, the morning's gloom added extra pizzazz to the atmosphere.

This place lent Claudia a bird's-eye view of the entire alley. A young baker came out of the café. At a pull of a wiry string hanging by the side of a wall, he flicked open the café's maroon awning with a white wavy line down the edge. It jutted over the pavement; water droplets dribbled out from the awning's open corners. Standing by the tall window, Claudia watched without any misgivings, the morning's fate unfold.

A flower shop stood next door. Wet flowers drooped in the heavy battering of the rain. Flowers rooted to their pots' black soils. A cluster of pots under the shop's white awning. A young flower girl rushed outside to take the pots indoors. She carried them, one pot at a time. She flitted in and out in a long, pink skirt and a mauve blouse. When she came back to collect more pots, her foot stumbled in her skirt's hem; she slipped and fell on her ankle on the wet cobbles. This caught the young baker's attention. He ran over to assist the girl and found out that she had a sprained ankle.

Claudia watched in earnest. The baker picked her up and brought her over into his boulangerie. He brought her a glass of water and some pills, which she took. Then he

153

made her the finest cup of coffee, Claudia imagined, and one for himself as well. They sat down under the soaking awning to have their coffee. It was like a Charlie Chaplin silent movie. Claudia fast-paced the events into quick rag-doll movements: Charlie wooing his girlfriend, standing up and then sitting down closely next to her; his arms angled around her neck. She didn't seem to mind. Then he brought his head down to her lips. She pouted her lips towards his. They kissed. Claudia watched this exciting moment of joy. They kissed and then they laughed. There was not a care in the world. The rain had not abated. Water gushed down the stormwater drain in the rivulet.

Then this otherness retracted. This dark side slowly crept into Claudia's mind: Miss Havisham in her bleak house, who had everything but starved of the companionship of the one true love. She owned everything, except her life. A life that passed her by, lost in the snitches of time. Claudia realised desperately that the baker and the florist must decide to be together. Life's full meaning must be harnessed in this togetherness. She must tell them Miss Havisham's tale. That they must not allow themselves to suffer the pain of a relationship breakdown, should they choose to decide otherwise. This sweet, sweet tale of love in the Parisian rain must not end in tangled masses of crisscrossed cobwebs.

She trod across her apartment floor, away from the windows towards an umbrella stand set along a brick wall. She picked up a transparent umbrella and set off. She ran down several flights of stairs, and out in the open on the pavement across the alley. She stood there under her umbrella and heard the soft swishes of the wind blow. She saw the rain's tiny drizzles on her umbrella's downturned dome. There they were, lying idle in each other's gentle embrace; they wooed and they cooed and they whispered delightful sweet nothings without a miss. The rain must go on. It was the rain that held the enigma of the moment. She must make the rain remain longer somehow. She stood there, yes Claudia, stood like the great giant Thor, her umbrella, her hammer in the Nordic god's immortal grips.

Something happened. Her thoughts collapsed like the switching off of a hologram projector. Claudia stepped out of character. No, it was she, who wanted to be the girl in the baker's arms. But not in the present, at a different time. She fell through a slit. She was with him, the baker in Louis' castle in Versailles. She wanted him all to herself. no. no wait. There was a revolution. The baker was taken prisoner from their cottage. He never returned.

But he did return to the florist. He fell through another time slit and here he was in the morning's rain. So did she. Oh! Where was the story going? The baker and the florist rose from the seats hand in hand. She looked up, her face in the rain. She laughed. He gazed at her beauty. Her laughter rang down the tapered alley leading the way to the couple's opaque destiny. The flowers smiled in the pots, dressed to dance in threaded petals of pink, and blue frocks. A picturesque array, while the rains showered glimpses of cosmic insights. Had there been no rain, then the girl would not have fallen, and coffee would not have followed. The baker and the florist would not have met. Events would not have transpired the way they did.

Claudia with her umbrella, Miss Havisham's memories from her days, the ghosts, a teasing thin wall of separation between her reality and this. The couple walked on. She watched them promenade and yearned for what was lost. On the timeline's linear path, many non-linear moments played out. The rain tapped away on the cobbles, the boulangerie, and the flower shop, a whiff in the wind of dust and sand. Music of a silent heart, a violin stringed to che sera whatever will be will be; Claudia's apparition was frozen in time, this long, indelible shadow of the bleak house birdlime.

First published by *Adelaide Literary Magazine*, Magazine 37, June Issue, USA, 2020

Wait for the Next Rain

Darkness crept in. Rain poured. I ran outside. I wanted to be with rain. No, wait, I wanted to rain-dance a tango. Night had fallen. Waters gushed. It whispered to make inroads into my soul. I opened up to it. I found my knight. He rode up in silver tresses and translucent shining armour. I embraced him. We kissed. My luscious lips, my satin face, my glassy eyes, and my wavering hair. He soaked me up in his wet embrace. He dripped down my wild hair. I closed my eyes and let it woo me. The rain stopped. The dance stopped. The romance stopped.

I came indoors in a brooding mix; I broke down in tears. I waited for the next rain. I awaited him.

Wait. Did I just find God in the Rain? My knight, all dispersed. Oxygen, nitrogen, and carbon, gathered and made us, humans. Fascinating, the rainbow colours. All the eye could see was us; God. He? Dispersed? We, humans, the God-gatherers, our skin was an outfit. Unzip the outfit, see the gatherings: all the Godly elements that the naked eye wished to see. Yet, each time we were born, we broke away from the stars and we created our own. Each time we died, the stars died with us to rise anew: helium, oxygen, nitrogen, all the droplets of the rainbow colours, transcendental idealism. God, the unbroken thread of life held us in the end, puppets on an eternal cosmic string.

First published by *Flash Frontier*, New Zealand, July 2020

Elysium

Today, no bullets were shot from any guns. No bodies were zipped up in body bags. This war-torn region hadn't had a break like this in fifteen years. The inhabitants of this place let out a sigh of relief. The war cries had stopped finally in a rare moment of munificence.

However, other kinds of activities were noted. These occurred internally within the human bodies. Vapid groans could be heard, but not from gunshots, sounds of morbid short breaths. They were unbeatable, foghorns sounding off tidings of grave unease. These could be termed as war also. In the throes of a different sort, where elements were engaged in a battle with an enemy within, they fought a fierce fight with the Invisibles.

A war that could not be mapped out geographically, but defined only in scans and x-rays. The enemy here chose to reside in throats and in the lungs, but mostly in the lungs. This was its post, where it lunged out an unscrupulous war. It choked its victims without a compunction until they became incapacitated and breathless. Fortuitously some lived, but many died. Those who died, they perished in multitudes, like gathered flies of the pestilence; this sinister battle, could not be pinned on any one nation or place, but littered through the globe. It didn't discriminate between kings, princes, paupers, heathens, or believers; it swept them all into the one crowded compartment of a boat, namely Elysium.

The crew of the Elysium knew the underworld well. The boat was anchored in an offing, as the war continued to scale up. It cleansed the world and this cleansing did not finish anytime soon. Fearful of the new enemy, people hid away wherever they could. They stayed indoors and did not see the light of day. For days on end, for weeks, and months, they feared this elusive enemy could drop in on their doorstep and get inside. People hoarded what they could. Shops were scarce of food, toilet paper, and antiseptic wipes. Religious leaders sermoned to empty halls of churches and mosques. Gregorian chants, sung in isolation, reached a zenith; a space, tuned up with high notes of a heavenly soprano. The forlorn street lamps lit up a ghost town, occupied only by bats and vultures. Now a mere shadow, billions of years of evolution seemed to have backtracked to the singularity of primordial darkness.

The enemy reigned supreme. By far, this was the most enigmatic enemy that had surpassed any mighty princes; this battle brought the human race to its knees and broke its hubris, this passing phase of a fragile ephemera. A task, which no other could accomplish with this level of dexterity. And they marched full on. This black swan soldiered on ruthlessly until the wake of a new dawn. A sun's reflection ponded on the waves of a misty, crisp beginning. Swans and geese flapped their wings and were raised in the ray's infancy. They didn't get wiped out, and neither did the bats, whose final flings ended this drama, a short while back.

_____

First published by *Flash Fiction North*, UK, April 2020

159

Debt

In a way, Natalie Kaye behaved like a dog. She succumbed wildly to tender love and care, a mild case of malady one may say. She had an accident once, a broken ankle. Kaye waited out this dent, with pent-up emotions. In and out of hospitals, she made several trips. People came forward to help her at home, while she was still ill in bed, alone and forlorn. These were Kaye's neighbours and friends from around her belt. After her recovery, when she became alert, she stetted a long list of names, who didn't rejoice in her bane. Be it with food, money, or cleaning, they paid her bills and fed her well.

Natalie felt she was in debt. One day though, who didn't grow, she put up a show, for her friends in tow. They waited in row, at cocks crow, for Natalie the pro to bow, slow and low. Lo and behold! There she was, her heart in her hands, asking for avenues to express her gratitude; pulling out weeds, planting new seeds, cooking their meals, even when they didn't want it. This was how she insisted on paying all of her debts, to all of her friends.

However, these were just the beginning of days. As if these weren't enough, Natalie Kaye was willing to lay under a starry sky; be an owl on a prowl, go on her neighbour's lawn, staying awake guarding it all night long. Time and time again, her neighbours said it was enough; and enough it sure was, but Kaye was undeterred. Then one day, they were furious and actually told her off. Not in so many words, expressed a lot of guff.

Blue at dawn and russet at dusk, Natalie's mood had become awry and brusque. She couldn't cope and did rue the day when she hadn't heeded her friends. They had said she had overdone. Today she looked at all the closed doors and thought maybe she needed to do less, not more. This taught her a lesson. How far should she have gone, to avoid falling out with friends at once? From then onwards, Natalie Kaye had not spoken a word but had become suicidal. Another fine day, a fire broke out; in this peril, she dragged herself out. With a pail in her hand, at the forefront of a public rant, Natalie stood along with this tumult. Then moments later, her friends were there; they stood abreast in a kindred spirit. It was the fire, which brought back her friends anew. Some of them were new. But, Natalie Kaye had learned it, although it was the hard way. She smiled and greeted, only when someone nodded. For she knew her limits and her off-limits. Natalie Kaye moved on, fared well under the same sun she shared with everyone.

The exploitation of Natalie Kaye was not in any way even on the horizon of her friends' imaginations. She lent herself so freely to them, that they could very well take advantage of her situation. Since they hadn't done so, Natalie Kaye found more reasons to owe. Her heart once again shifted and pumped gratitude, as she thought she needed to own up to them. But she had to strike the right kind of balance between too much and too little. She had to devise a ruse. How much was enough, she didn't know. She was a Sagittarius, ruled by power, well beyond her, the expansive Jupiter.

The ruse, she thought had to be one of a kind. She'd rather pay off her debts, only in this manner. She must not go overboard, with soaring emotional inroad; control of the mind was paramount. She reminded herself, fair and square, that Natalie Kaye, could keep both her cake and eat it as well. She locked herself in, yet once again. But this time she jumped on the internet. To chase her ruse, she found her muse and browsed online night and day. She stumbled into an arena, where she found a maleficent partner. She slipped literally into the dark web, which

161

overwhelmed her, by what she found there. This exposure brought something to light that, by far, was out of sight. She found a "plague doctor" selling human blood through the villages of England. Natalie Kaye, in her present mental state, nested more and more in the mire of this dark world web.

A ruse? A ruse? Of course, a clue in the cruise, but more like a bruise. Right here, given her nature, she became addicted to it. Drugs, illegal trafficking of human organs, and human blood are all sold, all in a day's work! All explored. A mystery woman, she turned to the dark web and found her ruse there which was most unexpected. The dark web pulled her in the same way that one would be touched hanging around the graveyard, grimly surreal. Perhaps there was insanity, who knew? But her goodness was turning, the pendulum slowly shifting at a blow of a whiff off the internet. Natalie Kaye was changing. Bend over backward, a tendency she always harboured, she roamed the net and often wondered. This otherworldliness, bitterly stygian, just as well her impulses were irrepressible. Anybody's guess what she'd do next, Natalie Kaye, in the grips of these low-life elements. Sell her body? Sell her organs? Sell her blood to her satisfaction, as she couldn't do in government hospitals? Nobody knew, not even what dark secrets she held deep within her cells. Forget the ruse! Forget payback! The sentient Kaye wasn't on the right track. A new ruse needed to be fused, to issue a new way to defuse this snare. Then, only then, she would have paid all her dues that she felt she needed to own up to friends.

"A long day's journey into night," Natalie was impossible to find. Grief made her friends blind. They held a meeting and decided to awaken Natalie that evening. As she hung out on the worldwide web, she heard knocks, sourly desperate. It wasn't an option to not open the door, she felt her dear neighbours were going to dig through the floor. She went up to the front when she realised with a grunt that the darknet on the computer was still turned on. She was at large, all these days, the same kindred spirits now barged in. They found out that she had been living in the dreary world of virtual reality. They talked her out of it. And pulled her out of the hole. They rescued her from a deadly mole, which could've caused her great woe. She thanked them duly from her heart, but her indelible debt mounted much. What was the long and short of it? That she couldn't deal with this debt and began to feel restive again. Natalie Kaye couldn't keep her emotions at bay.

First published by *Melbourne Culture Corner*, Issue 4, Australia, 2020

The Portrait

On the crossing of Victoria and Harriet Street stood a building of a massive block of grey apartments. Up in the front of each flat, balconies jutted out like open matchboxes, creating a blind spot for the incoming traffic. It posed an undeniable threat to the traffic on the road. Notwithstanding, the building had much to offer in the way of charm.

It would have looked quite stark, had it not been for the indoor plants. Some balconies had synthetic black chairs placed around a white table of six. Commonly, all the flats had plants of many shapes and colours. Bunches of scarlet geraniums, and white and yellow chrysanthemums hung over the balcony rails. Rows of vines reached out to the sky. Such motley colours are found in the early blooms.

An artist spotted the building. She took up her brush and painted it in nuanced detail. The building looked surreal on the canvas. She brushed a uniformly cold structure first. Then vastly varied human stories percolated within its walls. On a rainy day, when the clouds descended heavily, the building had a dull perspective, which gave it a grey, surreal look. Particularly, with an untrodden path running by it, vanishing midway out of vision. Little remained to be seen of the path except a few wet bamboo trees aligned on the edge of half a path, drooping tender shoots, and emerald green leaves. Either way, through rain and fall, cold and heat, the artist's rendition made it pale or bright, as wild as mood swings. However, the structure remained solidly rooted to the ground.

When her painting was just halfway through, the artist sat down to clean her brush. And then something struck her incognito. She put the brush away and picked up cans of paint one after another of pastel green, rhubarb red, "alentejo blue", and lavender purple, and splashed them vigorously on the canvas, nearly suffocating the building in a sea of callous colours. She panted as she did so. Sitting down afterwards, she reflected upon this idiosyncratic behaviour on the canvas. It was complete devastation. She painted a child's look of horror penetrating through the riotous colours, a mother holding the child's hand and desperately trying to make a quick getaway in utter panic. The artist conjured up an image.

She took up her brush and moved on to the next canvas. The hilltop of Harriet Street, where she stood, gave her a vantage point to look through the workings of the minds of the residents. Freakish thoughts of mad desires were being reshaped on the canvas. These appeared in the coloured waves of fuchsia pink, blood orange, and translucent lemon. As though she was painting the essential gases: nitrogen, hydrogen, oxygen, and the silken aurora borealis in a full spectrum of celestial colours to represent human love, rage, and sorrow.

Her eyes opened up to each apartment in a unique way: mothers cooking at the stove, girls watering potted plants on the balconies, lovers' entwined bodies kissing at dawn break, readers engrossed in the pursuit of philosophy, couples arguing followed by break-ups, children crazy with computer games, musicians playing pianos at evensong. Events happening all at once, every day, each on its orbit. There was no dearth of colour as she indulged herself in colour on colour. An inner reality of abstraction superimposed unhindered. And then the artist thought of the figurines on the Parthenon of the great antiquity.

Possibly, she could paint real people and bring them to life. And she did. She painted little figurines, residents of the apartments and brushed them with heavy strokes of colours, infusing life into them. They took their places now on the pantheon of life's theatre. Within the cold marble of

165

each insignificant apartment wall, human tales played out their significant dramas. Stories of happiness and misery, one too many, each told earnestly in various ways.

The artist now heard passionate outbursts. Life's veritable tales unfolded in casual conversations. "Why was she called that, 'Mowgli's mother'?" – a male figure, demanding to know why a certain person would be called so all through her life some four hundred years ago on this very soil? Who was Mowgli after all? Has anyone seen him say that she should be called so? He addressed some people, whose muteness suggested that even they did not know, who Mowgli was? Maybe Mowgli was an illegitimate child of this mother, whose identity was to remain a mystery forever; yet, Mowgli would be the one to have survived the test of time in a bizarre irony, even after four hundred years had passed. He would be remembered through a mother known only by that: "Mowgli's Mother" nothing more.

No one ever saw this boy. What was this mother's story after all? Mother of an unwanted child. In a four-hundred-year-old figurine, the artist was drawing a dancer, dancing for the Lord of a clan on a moonlit night. With flimsy cotton wrapped around her barely covered body, she was taken by the young Lord as his paramour. A baby boy was born. She was now seen breast-feeding it. The next depiction was of the Lord's men marching into her hut and snatching the baby away. The helpless mother cried out in pain; the seductive dancer of the young Lord was sent to exile. Here in the new land, she called herself, "Mowgli's Mother". To this day, she was known as "Mowgli's Mother".

What was the portrait all about? Tall tales told about every man and every woman, since the inception of human history. Old replaced by a new wave of life on this resolute earth. Within these walls of one's apartment, plants grew in a profusion of colours. The artist painted changes. A change had occurred indeed! Flowers from one of the pots died; in the same soil, a resident decided to plant tomato seeds to foster a different life, in a different moment.

_____

First published by *Straylight Literary Magazine*, USA, 2016

Bad Bone

The cafe hummed a note of non-rhythmic jingle. I sat with a glass of sparkling water reading Fitzgerald's *Tender is the Night*. Deep in reading, I took a sip occasionally. As it stands, the passages of infidelity bothered me more than the stylistic complexity of the book. It resonated with something that I did not wish to remember. A wind picked up just outside the glassed window. My attention diverted because of an intermittent, yet twiggy knock; a tall gum tree stood against the pane; a sudden blast tore off a branch and felled it on the sill. I looked at it briefly and resumed my study of the characters.

A sea of snow, the whispering winds of quietness. I reflected on a placid icy slope of a winter afternoon; silent like a still painting, my face stood out amongst the cafe crowd. Not a sore thumb, as there were others like me too, but with more sprightly, appealing demeanours. It eluded me. Carefree, I thought. Something tore me in the gut. I conferred with an inner self and tried to understand a joy colluded with despair. Not known to me, why had it always been like that. To not be able to separate the clashing emotions fused within the unmarked waves of the soul. My soul never at peace, oscillated between here and there; between a temporary world of the body and elsewhere, a life of the mind or the spirit. Of the mind, I noted with care. An inner self of being, where dreams took place, more so in hibernation.

Hibernation was the word. That was a long journey. It offered no reprieve from dreaming on a continuum. In awakening, the tall green grass now turned into straw. Dehydration caused hallucination. The letter was way too late, my fate could have turned. But no, that was not written in the stars. Love written off. I couldn't break someone's heart. Accepting the letter meant a defeat for Pat. Married, yes but she had married him, while his realisation of love for me came later. He was already married but full of dilemma. Pat never knew. Pat had nowhere else to go. He married her, then left her by herself. Long overdue. Forlorn, she didn't know what happened to him. I received his love letters, one too many. An imminent affair loomed at my doorstep and knocked me over. I read the letter but did not respond.

A marriage of the heart very well could have been. But the grass had been dehydrated by then. The dehydrated grass turned into straw. Then the brittle straw clung on to the earth for dear life. I went into quiet hibernation. Now there was a stream of straw whose tortuous roots lay rooted to the soil. The soil made of sand caved into its roots. Nurtured it not, the soil lay hollow. Then there was a hole. A hole in the soil where I slept in awakening and I dreamt of nothing. But hunger acted as fuel. A hunger I ate all day. I walked in a dream, the dream of life, listening to the spring birds that broke the silence of the morn. There was silence in my heart. It whispered, but a dirge. It was spring. Love in the air.

The air was fresh; I sat under an apple tree. Fresh red apples hung over me. An apple tree burdened with fruit. Burdened. My heavy heart was burdened by so many memories. If one could paint them, then there would be many shades of red. I buried myself deeper into the burrow, the hole which I clawed. I picked up the dirt with my own two hands. The dirt which slithered between the five fingers. It slithered right through. The waves of my thoughts flowed undulated. I wanted to see him now. After many seasons, I wanted to know what he looked like. I gave him up for Pat because she was a homeless orphan. I had given him away only to find him after all these years. Age and ageing broke me. Broken bones but not bad bones. Would it be bad to want him back in my life? I didn't have a single bad bone, they said. Alas! It was the paradox that killed me.

The poisoned ivy crushed me unduly. Creepers, the poison, crept up the spine. The love potion, at its best worked like magic, at its worst a delusion. Maybe, it was delusion. I never really wanted him. I was better off without him, perhaps. Leave him to his nemesis, to his Pat, one that he married, then he had second thoughts and wished that he had not married for he loved me. That was what he thought. And his thought turned in a while, and then he took Pat back. She was soft and sensitive. She used to say this world is too harsh, far too harsh. Yes, it perhaps was for her, who never cared to do much. I dug deeper into my trench. I dodged a bullet. It could have taken its toll. He would never have understood. Much too much, far more engrossed, with money and matter. I, on the other hand, soared on the wings of poesy. It would not have worked out for me. A realisation, it was better this way. I pulled myself up, out of the burrow. The leaves under the tree, crunchy and brown.

Brown, a natural process of decay; brown, because it paved the way to new life. The dehydrated grass had turned into straw when I hibernated. Now the straw turned back into green grass. I felt content. Shades of pink turned my reds around. I felt not just content but young again. I was a sheaf of corn, the life-giving properties of the sun and sprinklings of water. Back to the waves where life began as did hope and optimism. Optimism and hope replaced the drought of the soul and the nihilism of my thoughts.

—————————

First published by *Ellipsis Zine*, UK, 2019

Elusive Love

Shamshi Rahman didn't have enough money to put meals on the table. He had recently lost his job. The only way to raise quick funds was through friends online. He sat looking through his Facebook page every day to find potential givers. Some of his friends were too young to afford any charity. Older friends looked cashed up. He focussed on them. He found one.

An elderly woman, but she looked young. He thought he would stalk her. Shamshi began pandering to her love instincts. He sent her little love notes. He complimented on her looks, and then her curvy figure. It was all very mechanical, trying to grab her attention. How to make someone fall in love, kind of "How to" manual books, which he thought were useful. General love and lovemaking tips.

Her name was Claudia Hanson. She was much older – at least thirty years between them. He told her that he loved her. He had always been in love with her. But his courage failed him to ask her. She told him that it wasn't going to work because of the age difference. He said he didn't care about age. Every time he saw her, he felt his loins stir. He couldn't live without her. He couldn't breathe without her. He desired to live within her.

She told him she loved no one. She had a cold, cold heart. She was like a broken record on a decrepit player. She was like an aged palace or a mossy old temple half-devoured by some unknown thousand-year-old tree. That she was Homer's Red Wine Sea. She breathed old, stale air of the past and the present and perhaps a bit into the future too.

But Shamshi was indomitable. He wrote back, If I compare thee to a summer's beach, then I'd reflect on its rippled peach. The golden sand which time could never reach. It's pretty, pristine ripples preserved like the clenched newborn fist, saw billions of years come and go, but never touched the sands to bleach. However, sandcastles may break. Mandalas wiped off. Children played, past, present, and future. The time had moved on. But the beach remained without a blemish. The sea by its side, carrier of bloody bodies, pirate histories, papyrus battles. Homer passed on. His Wine-dark Sea remained just the same. A new day was issued. A fresh face of youth. New creases appeared on the skin once it was smooth. Unchangeable and unwrinkled, but, time over time. Sands soaked up human dramas played over it. I sit here on the sand today. I sat here many moons ago. I shall continue to sit until I break my bones. Time will never touch me. Time touched the great Ozymandias. Futile. But the sands proved more powerful than all. Time stood still at its edge without a stir. For this was love, the sand of unbroken looping nerves.

He video-conferenced with her. He told her that he wanted to make love to her online. His endless desires would never melt. She told him no physical relationship. He told her it wasn't physical. It was all spiritual. It was esoteric. She was an embodiment. His prism of love. That was incredulous. She told Shamshi that she wanted to end it; thirty years too late. But she felt a mad rush of love too. One that she couldn't understand. She couldn't get him out of her head. She even told him that. But Shamshi kept reminding her that love had to be nurtured in the heart, not in the head.

She felt love for no one. She was an empty shell. It had been empathy. She had compassion. But never love. She tried to convince Shamshi that love for her was a losing battle. She would never win it. Shamshi asked her to feel it.

He told her to feel love inside the heart. Meet him online. She held herself back. She tried to forget this had ever happened. It was impossible. She read his words. Etched the lines in her heart. They were unforgettable. She wanted to be with him. But he had also asked for money. He had asked her to send some funds through. Perhaps he needed it, but this impurity had already touched the sand. Its fang of suspicion went deep.

He was using her. She felt used.

But Shamshi told her otherwise. He told her, there was no impurity as far as love went. Money was incidental. It was never going to tarnish it. She almost believed him. She did because he was inside of her too. His words, his poetry held her spellbound. This was love. This was not love. He was there. He was not. He spoke in poetry. He spoke in riddles. After all, what was the heart of the matter? Where was all this going to end? They were tied. Knotted together despite the impurity. Money. He used her. He used her not. He drained her. He drained her not. He gave her immense pleasure, but bankrupted her – emotionally, financially, mentally.

She was losing it. She was not. She was sinking. She was not. Enchanting. It was not. She was at war. There was a pandemic. The physical meeting was impossible. But this pandemic had not diminished his desire. As he continued to sweet talk romance into her ears, she became more and more aware of his presence in her heart. She began to feel less empty. Then again that was just her. She had no idea how this played up on Shamshie's end. When she asked him how he felt about her, he replied to what she wanted to hear. That he was her friend, her lover, her life. That she meant everything to him. She fell for it. She wanted to believe him. He convinced her. She started to send him even bigger amounts in cash, thinking what if he died from starvation? She had to give him the benefit of the doubt. How else was she going to live without him?

One day, she went up to his Facebook wall. She scrolled up and down for more information. She came across a post. It said something about marriage. She read it carefully. It was about a marriage proposal that Shamshie was discussing. He planned to propose marriage to someone. Her heart missed a beat. She continued to read it. All the congratulatory comments made her sick in the gut. She got off. She couldn't sleep that night. There were no calls from Shamshie either. The next morning, she woke up with heartache. She had been such a fool. She logged on to Facebook and found a picture of a wedding ring in her messenger. Surely an invite from Shamshie; how dared he? She looked into the note which came with an image. It astounded her. "Claudia, marry me."

First published by *Love in the Time of Covid: A Chronicle of a Pandemic*, New Zealand, January 2021

Rag

Consistency wasn't my forte. I watched my parents play chess every day with a tad of scepticism, thinking if they enjoyed playing the same game. My mother could win hands down. My father lost every time. It upset him. He was a bad loser. Just watching them was monotonous. The same arguments over those moves on the chessboard.

In those days, I wore Naagras. They were royal shoes with a narrow pointy front bow. I went to some dark places in them. Both boredom and romance took me into forbidden forays, as I sought newness. I didn't know what I expected. A nuanced romance that would explode a life of taste and colour. The more I tried, the more disappointment my adventures brought me flat prairies of no exciting relationships.

One summer's afternoon, however, I sat reading Tagore's *The Last Poem*. His definition of love and marriage eluded me. The essence of true love is fascinating and dangerous, he compared true love with an ocean where the mellow heart must be allowed to immerse occasionally. Marriage, on the other hand, was washed away with sullied water, fetched every day, and used every day.

Then I heard footsteps. Our neighbour's son Sunny ambled through the garden. I looked up. He smiled and sat down next to me. We started talking about romance and marriage.

"Are you reading Tagore's *The Last Poem*?"

He asked looking at the turned pages.

"Yes," I answered.

"How are you liking it?"

"I like his views on love and marriage," I said.

"Hmm, Interesting take. Say, do you think Madame Bovary could change?" he asked.

175

"Seriously? No, I don't think so. Her boredom was too deep."

He noted my terse answer. However, I continued unabashed.

I had roped myself in defence of the Madame Bovarys of the world. Suddenly, Sunny looked at me strangely. He pulled me towards him. His lips were pressing hard and hot on mine. I had the strangest vision in his arms. I felt a connection. Something clicked.

"I have been there. Done it, many, many times."

I cried and unlocked myself from his arms.

"With the same person?" he asked.

"No."

"Aha," he chuckled.

I started to walk away from him. He followed me. We entered the house together. Our parents chatted on the far side of the veranda. Sunny joined them for a drink. I went to my bedroom and stood by the window. The pomegranate tree was in full bloom. True love didn't exist, I reminded myself. But, I felt something there with Sunny, which I had not felt with any others. Maybe Sunny checkmated me. Maybe, I was in love. One kiss, could this transform me? I braced myself for a fall.

The next day, I woke up. I thought of Sunny's kiss. The first thought of the day was this that I was eager to see him today. I texted him asking for a date. He responded promptly. It was in the afternoon again in our garden shed. Time appeared to have moved slowly this morning. But the moment arrived. I went up to the garden shed. I saw him from a distance, waiting for me under a tree shade. He grinned at me. I grinned back. I pulled up a branch of a mango tree as I walked under its foliage.

I had walked a few steps towards him and he walked towards me. We met halfway. He kissed me again and refreshed my memory of his last kiss. A desire swelled in my heart. He carried me and he walked towards the shed. As we entered it, I realised that he had come prepared with soft linen and pillows to make it all comfortable.

After about a quarter of an hour, I saw through the tiny shed window, a crow flying in and sitting on the shed of the corrugated iron roof. He dropped a patch of faeces on its edge before it flew away with a caw. Sunny and I spent nearly two hours here. That was just the beginning of a romance. He recited sweet poems that he had written. He poured them into my ears so my cold, cold heart of short-lived romance would melt to submission. I began to feel it, the passion, the romance, and a rash desire for Sunny. Sunny was the one, the only love of my life.

Some moments passed in silence. I thought of love, then I thought of the crow too, flying here from nowhere for a release. Sunny looked at me and asked. "What's up! What're you thinking?"

"Of you," I answered.

"Really? Do you want to marry me?" he asked in earnest.

"Yes, I do."

"Hmm."

"Hmm? I asked.

"Not sure, if you're committed enough."

He lit a cigarette and made a smoky ring as he puffed it out through his pouty lips. The penny dropped for me. Sunny was right. I wasn't ready for marriage. Marriage was a mirage. When the passion relinquished, I realised I was another Madame Bovary: another tragedy in waiting.

First published by *Ellipsis Zine*, UK, May 2021

Chasing a Dream

I am old. But I wear a slippery, silken skin without a single crease. I carry a great many twigs, logs, and sodden leaves. I bear boats and swords and house swordfish, home to spoons, plates, and glasses. Gold, and silver of priceless trinkets. I witness listless stories of storms and floods. Human dramas played out upon my waves. Great tragedies, even comedies sometimes. Wavering upon my breast, cherished ephemera, jewelled bridal cavalcade of lost arks. Destruction of land, giving way to the new land across the other side. New farms yellowing, new laughter ringing, new loves budding, on the far stretch of the alluvial deposits.

Then one day, the drama takes a turn as I bend around the lofty gums. All is going smoothly on the precious, fine land. A branch falls off with a thud. Splosh, Splish, Splash. I cave in, a moment, pirates are on the run.

A sepulchre is lowered. It touches the bottom of my gut. That the pirates mutter, not enough, not enough is taken from the new land maiden. Homes have been ransacked. Jewellery in the casket, bales have been torched, and people burnt alive. Yet, that is not enough, the weighty sepulchre, more gold, and more silver on the horizon. My body is murky and heavy in places. Dark and grim, sorrow is painted. In my burrow, I see what I see, I hear thee, I bury all your grievances and I record them below. I record, not recoil, but vengeance is mine.

A cyclone slaps hard, a catcher in the rye. The pirates on the lurch, take them up in the madness of ruckus. They flee as far as they can. But the eye chases them until dawn. It takes them astride. The pirates are funnelled and then embedded, not far from the sepulchre. This is the story, I take back to the maiden, who is still waiting in the white bereaved garment. It has happened. Now you can move on.

Make new jewellery, even more, fashionable ones. The maiden hears me out. But she says nothing. And I wonder, why this news has not sunk at all. The sun has risen. Vultures have flown away. The time is now ripe to chase the dream of life. Start life anew.

The divine numbers, 1,2,3, and 4 are pure and wilful. They do what they do. They slide, and never look back. Use it. This window of opportunity may not return. Pirates are gone and will not be coming along in a long, long time now. I cannot wait for I am the tide of both glad tidings and bad. I proceed unhindered. I mope for loss. When the bridge is crossed, over the moss, I see an albatross. Oh no no! The maiden is cursed. No rhyme, no reason. They said she brings bad luck. A community of fools has decided that and they condemned her to distrust. No happy ending, this tale ends here. My nuanced waves cannot be euphoric. No winds to stir them now. No big ships foghorn. My waters were placid, as the maiden's body surfaced.

First published by *Door is a Jar*, 18th Edition, Spring Issue, USA, 2021

Ylem

Her name was Andromeda. She swam on satin water. Lapped up in the silk, her mind was restive. Her thoughts were agile but discrete and nonlinear. Absorbed her musings, her dreams were clear. She swam in them, out of her depth; just as well, they kept coming back. Braided in and out, oscillating, and edgy, they chased her almost, inconsequentially. In a way, her swim impeded these half-formed thoughts, writ on water's hem.

In the aftermath of the war, random bodies floated. Down by the stream which eucalyptus skin coated. Covered by stringy barks, pale faces were spotted. The enemy gloated; bodies were quite bloated. Marked with agony, of the swollen bodies, some eyes shut, peculiarly, some were still open. Her focus turned in a moment.

She sat next to her mother. They chatted in an oval room, mother and daughter. Her mother looked fresh and young, way back, a maiden. Andromeda was born much later.

She asked, "Where have you been all this time?"

"I had been out to a conference," her mother replied.

"How did it all go?"

Her mother answered, "Very good. All was good."

"Ah, but I missed you. I really did."

Her mother smiled. Father entered the room. His handsome face was radiant; the atmosphere lightened. Mother rose to offer him her chair. But father took a stool, sturdy and bare. Father died nearly a decade ago, Andromeda thought in retrospect. The room darkened. Over the water, bold and low, fluttered a lorikeet, a flying rainbow. It seemed it was going to gouge her eyes. But the sprightly bird frolicked, passing her elbow.

The neighbour, who like a father, died indeed. She went

to his funeral with a wreath. Then he dropped by to meet her that night, this reverie. She felt it was right to ask a question. "Have you seen God?"

"No," he replied. This, a silent place. Where am I? This present moment. Vast, and void, this light space, offers no air. Did I die? Am I dead?"

"No, God then?" she asked.

"Where is He? He hasn't come to meet me, yet," said the respondent.

"Do you miss us?" she had asked.

Tears in her dreams, she felt surreal.

"Yes, I miss your aunty," he answered, then he vaporised like a collapsed star.

A fusion of elements, hydrogen, and helium, led to the birth of a cosmic star. The helium ran out. Star collapsed. He collapsed. She saw the neighbour, driving his car through the suburbs of his choice, with his wife, whom he referred to, as aunty. The chemicals conferred. An accident occurred. He died. Of her dreams. Finite lives are made of infinite gasses, of the cosmos, of the elements; life perished. Andromeda contemplated the stuff of life. This precious breath, did it not live outside the orbit of death? Helium, hydrogen, oxygen, iron, and zinc.

Mountain passes were rugged. She walked through the terrain. A storm picked up, she looked for a spot. She found a cave. In the dark shelter, she sat amidst litter. A bolt of lightning fell outside. That creepy light opened her mind to shadows below. She was not alone; somebody was there. In a flash, the shadow disappeared. She was out of her wits. She tried to sleep. Just when she saw some cave paintings. On the wall, they looked ancient. And they were ancient. In a bit, she saw a little boy.

Broken charcoal in his hand, he sketched stirring stories, like the fall of Troy. He lit a small fire. Lights

181

emanating from the fire helped this sentient boy to see better. He drew stick figures of many shapes and sizes: tall, short, men, women, and children. It was almost dark, on the rugged wall, the shape of the boy silhouetted in the moonlight. Floodlights in the dark cave, paintings of tall tales, some washed up partly in the rain. A segment of a story, like this painting of an alley, people walked through with missing hands or hair. Many were even defaced in the falling rain. Colours ran down the leaves of trees and turned them into lighter shades of green. Pure paintings filled the dingy walls, and onto the floor, some scribbles crawled.

Gallows hung without much peruse. Kings devised a horrendous ruse. Spilled blood into the soil to infuse. Children sacrificed, for the fertility of the soils, far better use. With heavy harvest at stake, people kept quiet, with no one to refuse. Little boys to be taken, gods to be appeased. The King's men marched and dragged the boy away. Off to the gallows. Off with his head. The artist, little boy, broke into shreds. In white loincloth, wrapped around his waist, the boy's gaping horror clouded his face. His small hands trembled. She looked through a portal. Tears, and cries of the innocent sacrifice. No one took pity at the bloody altar. Wounds remained unaltered. Cosmic parameter, a stern factor.

Flashbacks played wistful memories; she lay on a beach a mere bystander. A silent witness to the many silken dreams, lovers entwined a beautiful beginning. Sunken sands, in waxed moonlight. Of the mandala, an ephemera, imperfect finale of the drama; done and redone until time had spoken, given up on the beach, a part of the resurrection. In the hours all became sand, quintessentially minuscule, and indestructible. In the heart of it, each wave flows, an atom of H_2O.

Over those swelling waves, she boarded a pirate ship. And saw a thousand vessels, a war imminent. On the horizon, a ship appeared like a phantom. A skeleton of a ship, spectacularly luminous, shone in the lantern. There was a gunshot fire. She was hit. Oh! It hurt! She was hurt.

She felt the pain of the gunshot. But she lived. She saw ships pass by, while her own cruised towards the nearest beach; seagulls scoured the skies. There were sands, the most wondrous, where monks built palaces and played Kings and Queens. Of a greater imagination, ruled by them, the three Moirae sisters. Monks made mandalas, painstakingly intricate, human history and destiny pleached. Giant pyramids were erected with care, and the Taj-Mahal, The great Ozymandias, the King of Kings, his life-sized statue pitched on the beach, immortalised in the scroll, the statue awash, the mandala destroyed, flattened to the ground.

The hollow sand; into the sand, she buried her legs deep to the waist. A hybrid form of part sand and part flesh. At its best, a mermaid's tail; she lay half-covered under the clay. High on her imagination, her dreams displayed decrepit old castles' and windows' deep splays. Such was the beach, on the edge of which, the tireless seas creased. Where romantics rode unicorns, nomads, wild horses, Homer, churned verses, now depleted.

Time's most valued, gift offerings to gods, watched this once how their altars burnt? Stars burnt out. The sun burnt. This gleaming altar was made out of gold; plush gold clouds nestled the thrones. A toy boat marooned, on a gold-plated sheet, uncertain of directions, an aluminium plate; hot liquid gold poured into the mould, this sea basin, replete to the brim. God's own altar, never to erode, shimmering and sure, until pilgrims came home.

Andromeda swam, a big hand bagged a snake. There was a man though towards dawn. He told her this and expressed a wish that he wanted to leave, to be born again.

"Born again?" she asked.

183

"Yes, that is possible," he said.

"Impossible. Because for you to remain what you are, you need genes from both parents."

"It is possible, though," the man said.

"What about your wife?"

"What about her?"

"Does she have a say in any of this?" she asked.

"Probably not."

The wife loomed. But she didn't seem to mind. She heard his desire. So, she did not hinder it.

On a fevered night, in one short month, the man left for a forest of illuminated fireflies. The blue forest sparkled, and a pathway was strewn, with sprinklings of fire ubiquitously flown. Around tall trees and slim short bushes, he walked alone through a lucid forest. A forest transformed into a conduit, this hermit of a man, roamed its bent unit. Reincarnation on his mind, the soul in another body, stars in the sky, twinkled a smile.

Here she was, with this lady in white, appearing in her dream, that's how it transpired. With some syringes in her hand, lips wet from betel juice, glowing with health, she stood at her bed. Holding them out, those long syringes, she knocked into her worldly senses.

"Your mother's injections."

"What?"

The lady vanished. Her mother had run out of insulin and was on the brink of a disaster. The lady had come to tell her this, to ask her if, she could get her some insulin. Andromeda's grandmother, this dear lady, kind and godly, rests now sadly. The silken waters blanketed her skin. Her swimming undeterred held her by a spell. This undying chemical, once produced within her organ, the failing pancreas, was now injected for survival.

"I've come to say goodbye," it seemed he taunted. She

looked at her brother, then understood his intent. Upon waking, she found it to be true, that this saintly priest had passed away too. This dreamland, not entirely unreal, of sense perceptions, was a parallel world. Sight sounds and smell, shaped up to be real, pain compounded a curious blend.

Disjointed thoughts came to pass. Mesmerising chimera seeped. Tantalising glimpses of enormous replica, as a shaded entity. Who's to know, what's with the truth, this wakeful life of actuality? A dream within a dream; a doll within a doll, within a doll, the picture awry, always off-limit. That cave painting in the rain, defaced people who walked up the streets, the greens washed off. Waters dribbled over, a partial reality, conceived by this artist in utter antipathy.

Such fragmented cognisance, a manifold layered dream, alluded to the allegory of the cave theme. Half a dream, a broken thought, the unfinished story, manifested in Plato's shadow reality. This palpable existence, transcended truth and hinged on puppeteers beyond familiar scope. Answered with certitude, flung within the stars, lay a larger image, the fate of the universe. The long and short of it, dismantle the stars, dismantle Leda, a sense of foreboding descended Andromeda. For, "It is the stars, the stars alone, that govern our condition," Shakespeare foretold.

First published by *Ginosko Literary Journal* Issue 24, USA, 2019

Cenote

Before the tell-tale stick figures of shinned solid bones, a priest sermoned. Etched on a Mountain cave of russet walls, in the pale shadows of a moonlight tall, a tale came to pass. That a famine had struck hard, a terrible pestilence followed. The rain gods must be appeased. They had to be cleansed. Innocent bodies were sacrificed. For there were no rains, certainly no grains. Undeterred by the crucifixion, this was the temple's ruse to boost harvest. The King of the land sat reading from a scroll. It was in the scroll of the dead, where this light was shed. A high price was at stake, the Sacred Cenote, where the heads were laid, within its magical orbit.

Children queued up in short loincloths. When they heard the divine decree, they were in awe. That the priest picked up a child and he took him to the gallows. Parents witnessed petrified, sunken souls in hollows. Little bodies lay at gods' altars. The severed heads were in chaos, but still no crops, nor any flying swallows. The famine persisted for yet another year. A gaping horror of cries, hollering justice to rise. But Nature remained mute. A silence played out. Like this cold marble of unheard, untuned lute.

Preservation of life was all the King cared about. His Queen gave birth to a boy, the future King. He was a father; he felt a sense of pride. His conscience gave him a choice, all babies including yours, or none at all to die at the altar of grains. It was his choice, the King's call. He thought. Then he thought again. Preservation of life was all he thought he cared about the most. Who's preservation? His baby's or the babies of his subjects.

First published by *Perception Magazine, Syracuse University*, Vol XXI Issue 37, USA, Spring 2021

Sparky

In a jaundiced sky, bats and crows flew amok in uncertain directions at dusk. The sky was a dark canvas of jittery flight. Ablaze over the tall gum trees was a tell-tale sign, suggesting the end of time. The fire grew. The denizens of the forest ran deeper around the bend. Human voices carried distress. Trees and houses and the animal habitat, all burnt to a cinder. The fire rose without reprieve. A permanent haze descended. Luminous sparks like ubiquitous fireflies bejewelled this feral frontier.

A boy braided in and out of charred trees looking for his dog.

"Sparky, Sparky, where are you, buddy?"

He called again through a thick haze. He heard a cry. The boy ran towards the whimper. It kept getting further away. In the meantime, the fire engulfed a quarter of the forest. The boy was tired by now. He stopped running. He found a well and sat down near it. It wasn't the thirst that made him rise. He heard that whimper again. Maybe, Sparky jumped into the well. The well water was murky. It appeared undrinkable, tasteless. He couldn't see anything in it. But heard intermittent whimpers behind a tall poplar.

"Sparky, is that you?"

The boy followed the whimpers. Fire sparks crackled, as a branch of the poplar fell. He walked straight through the fire. He saw Sparky on the outer edge, a blue fluorescence in a blue forest. Sparky's tail wagged when he saw the boy, a blue fluorescence. No more burns, no more thirsts, no more residues of dead memory.

First published by *Free Flash Fiction*, UK, October 2020

Rose's Lament

Daddy dad! Oh what am I to do now? Malcolm? No no nothing! He is but a baby No Oh this! This despair. Unbearable pain. The loneliness. But Malcolm is still small. Who? What am I to do? Quiet. Listen! Listen to the music. It is but the music of silence. For life has completely gone out of him. Grey lips, pale. He is so pale. Frozen like the still snow topped mountain. His body cut out to melt. Pulverise in grave. Eaten away by moths of... days go but nights... Oh how dark is it? How dark is it in that grave? Peter, Peter can you hear me? The coffin to be lowered. Swollen like a belly full of water, the river flowed. The shimmering silver but look something sails it sails but not in isolation. Multitude of swollen floating. Floating like fallen leaves and the thin stringy water dripping barks of the poplars. Wake up! Peter please wake up. Look at our Malcolm. How he thrives in health... Who would take over Peter? All this wealth! The gold! Yes the gold. Who would run the business now? Malcolm can't! I can't either. John? What does he know? He doesn't know business.

Oh but you were never there. Look at me. Look me in the eye and tell me how was I to cope? Those lonely days have silenced our lives. Yours and mine, infidelity! That was it wasn't it? But I ran on the beach. I flung myself on the sand. I sink. Peter hold me. Pull me up. For I'm lost without you. I never knew I was so helpless. Have you seen God? Have you seen my two mothers. Emma and Lydia. Speak to me Peter please. Show yourself to me? Have you entered the heavenly nether-lands of death?

Life thrives beautifully in a never ending stream. Where there is no pain, no death, no fear. But is it me? is it really me in that kingdom of heaven? Peter I have questions for you. One too many to ask God. Eternal life. What would that be? The ocean in the front. Shimmers of dark water of odra… not down that way? Acheron? The river of pain. Through the powerful lenses of the lighthouse but… the Cocytus. The wails never end. They never do… When will I see you Peter? Will you come in my dream? There I see… I see you now… a shadow… an apparition… come to tell me how I failed. That strong smell of the skin balm. I can smell your odour. Your body odour does not beguile me. But oh, it does round and round the Oceanus. The laments of the widow down the Phlegethon down the depths of Tartarus.

First published by *CaféLit*, UK, October 2018

Phantom War

There are no real leaders, no real leadership; weapons won't cut it. Children of Gaza wake up to a discordant sun for they also know that they won't make it. They go hungry for yet another meatless day while ravens and crows scour over the hapless on red fields instead of yellow hay. Plenty lay under the rubble of this bay.

Fear and despair fuel the eastern coast of the Mediterranean Sea, unfolds a monumental catastrophe of biblical order; biblical it sure is. Gunpowder darkens a world, hearkens to the world's oversight, waging a phantom war. Where is the enemy hidden? Has the enemy fallen? As it unfolds 'tis just the children's bodies scattered in the dirt, bodies both big and small. Wrapped up in loincloth, white and dull; God forbid the coffin cloths should run out rendering the bodies exposed: mangled, and mingled in dirt. In Huxley's words: *Eyeless in Gaza,* a biblical story of the mammoth Samson and Delilah.

Seduced by Delilah, Samson was taken captive and handed over to the enemy. The Philistine people back in the day: people who migrated to the strip from the Island of Crete. The Philistines had gouged Samson's eyes as Samson becomes eyeless and powerless in the city of Gaza. Trapped and claustrophobic like the children of today.

Should Gaza rise again; should lyrical legends be told again; Don Quixote at the windmills?

Should Gaza be poetry again, should Gaza survive today's carnage, monstrosity of such a proportion? The children of Gaza, they didn't die for nothing. Gaza would survive by manyfold, the test of time fifty-thousand years to come and more. For Gaza is eternal. Gaza is Huxley's poetry. Gaza is simply that; poetry doesn't die.

First published by *Fevers of the Mind*, USA, 2024

Vape

Rozie vapes, tanning in a high afternoon sun in a skimpy bikini, lounging by the roof-top pool on her tall apartment building. She scrolls through the social media as she relaxes, surveying her skin every now and then, lavishly applying sun screen on her long hands, legs and the upper body portion. Her white skin slowly browns into light almond. She smiles as she reads the daily posts. Her lips spreading until her pearly teeth are showing a mystery simper, coining the corners.

She receives a call and speaks in a foreign language. She laughs and changes position in the lounge chair. Taut bare body, her limps are smooth. She splays her legs every now then to get sunlight into the inner thighs. Then she turns over and lies on her belly to let her back get full exposure to the sunlight. Her upper body and head inclines, propped up on the forehands under it. Still, scrolling her iPhone at the same time.

It is the sunlight she seeks to bask in it. The light caresses her bottom, her sinewy arms as it also speaks to her in a way that no one else understands. She closes her eyes and looks at the sun and communicates with it which only the sun understands. Her phone rings again. She exhales a few vapid smokes into the air, before she picks it up. She speaks in the same foreign language, like before.

A good fifteen minutes of monotone talk. Her pitch rises. She changes position, stretching on her back. However, she is yelling and crying instead of laughing, this time. The sun tries to appease her, bestowing warmth upon her slim waist, and rounded buttocks, flat midriff. But it fails to placate Rozie.

She is clearly unsettled. The sun moves and so does the warmth. Considerable shade descends on her warm body which is starting to feel cooler. Much cooler. She trembles slightly and hangs up the iPhone, frowning. She murmurs in her tongue as though she is talking to the sun.

"Mum thinks forces are conspiring against us. She thinks we, my boyfriend and I, split up because of some cosmic force preventing us. Who cares what happens to me? He was clearly cheating on me, banging other girls in front of me. Does it not hurt? I ask. Or is it supposed to turn me on, seeing him like this?

"Mum says boys will be boys. That's what they do. You tolerate. Yeah, right, who decides that? Like who decides what one must wear? I can wear next to nothing, or cover from head to toe, or wear no makeup; either way my life, my choice, no? I say, hell, yeah.

"Mum says I gotta wear more make up, I gotta look pretty, desirable for boys' eyes. She also says, I gotta cover up for that's what men want from pure women. I don't do any of that; that's why my boyfriend runs away. He flirts with girls who present themselves to be more desirable. Like you are running away, sun. I'm all cold and shivery. I could chase you all day, yet not get enough of you."

The sun responds, transiting notches away, farther this time. Rozie vapes a few more puffs and sits up. She wraps herself waist down with a slit saffron sarong. Her top part mostly bare, can barely keep up with the tremors.

"It's cold." She picks up her bag, stands up on her two bare feet, and walks out of the shade to pursue a new psychedelic sun, another day.

———————

First published by *Mad Swirl*, USA, March 2023

The Ceaseless

Paralysed from waist down, if Ash can't sell cow's milk, then there's nothing much he can do. His son tends the cows and sells milk at the bazaar for him. Sweet treats are made from this milk. Except, his pains persist. But he cannot resist but crawl down to the cowshed today to see a new fledgeling calf born. He watches the cow as it gives birth, while it growls in pain, the calf struggles and slithers out – a breath of fresh air.

The thunder god complains from his closed temple doors that while he hearkens to people's darkened hearts, he is not remembered much. Perhaps, once in while with some deference as a point of reference to pantheon of all gods without any offerings to the altar, songs or dance, his cosmic powers wan. The rain maker who brings fertility to agrarian lands may very well be crumbling biscuits with a lightning strike. Should the cowshed burn in his fiery hands, it will jeopardise the economic pipeline until Ash and his son can save up to buy another? This fledgling calf shares the shed with her mother. Ash's skin-deep wisdom makes his possibilities limited but knows this much that without the cow, he will not survive, just as without rains crops will not grow.

However, a deep existentialist paradox threatens the god of thunder which is that while he is reduced to a dot in the minds and the imaginations, the milk-seller thrives. Today, though, there is a coffin below. A wife bathes it and covers the deceased in a blanket because she shrinks to think that the dead must be feeling odd in those petrified, cold bodies – one short life to live.

Despite his pains, Ash's optimism grows. He trusts his cow is his saviour, and the crops. He can see them, feel them and eat them for sustenance. He loves the rain which brings fertility to the agrarian society. They are his real gods. What does he know? His wisdom is only skin-deep. Surely, the ceaseless thunder god knows better. Or does he?

Ash drags himself to the calf and rubs his hand over it. He picks a name, Pinky. Pinky sucks the mother's udder for milk, but before it is done, Ash's son comes along and extricates Pinky from his mother's udder and starts milking the mother in a bucket. Once the bucket it full, he takes it to the bazaar. Ash looks on at the hungry calf which tries the suck up the dry udder for more milk, but not one drop comes out.

Mother groans, the fledging groans, Ash groans. He understands the pain only too well which no god can cure, no matter how many times he may have prayed. Thousands of years of devotion wouldn't change a thing; a cog in the maker's system, yet the thunder god rages over the fact that it loses devotees by the minute, and he ceases to exist. The god sees his own face in that coffin.

First published in *Flash Fiction*. *Impspired Magazine* Issue #30, UK, 2024

a circle of fifths

Pale morning – Qasida singers walk through the deserted alleys, drumming up a traditional song of sehri in old Dhaka, "Wake up – it's sehri time. Get going, eat up, fast for Ramadan." Rifaat yawns and gets out of bed. She eats an early breakfast. After sehri, a distant tune of the azaan drifts from the minaret of a local mosque. The azaan distances Rifaat; in another era, another place, a spritely young girl named, Safina.

5:53 – a pale morning – Safina wakes up. She can't wait to be with Raja. Her Raja, or King, he certainly was; gilded he was not. Without a kingdom to rule, or any gold throne to ascend, people crowned him in their hearts, even when they mourned. For he was the "People's King," which everyone called him. Hence, Safina also called him that: "Raja". He was king of a kind who supervised spices, silk and trinkets that traversed down the Silk Road to western towns, trading ladies' gowns amongst other things. No merchant could ever pass without paying Raja their dues. He called it "taxes for the poor", regardless of whether they were friends or foes. Come to think of it, he was pretty poor himself; no trace of gold could ever be found in his crumbling shack, musty roof, or under his old cracked plank of a floor. Pots and pans had to be pushed under each leak in the roof to catch the drips of rain from many a monsoon.

However, every time Safina saw him, her heart soared for reasons unknown; she simply desired to be in his company, she would be by his side immediately while he stood at the checkout point, stopping and taking coins. Merchants made good money, so it was no big deal to give some to him. Other regulators also took a cut on every caravan passing down the track. They pocketed and amassed wealth in no time; no traders along the spice road could pass without paying. Unlike them though, Raja continued to live under the shaky roof of his nearly broken den.

"What do you do with all this money?" Safina asked him once.

"Come with me, I'll take you somewhere."

It was the month of Ramadan; without anything to eat or drink, they embarked on a journey down the Silk Road, an hour's horse ride towards the East. They arrived at a mountain range circling a small green lake, a veritable paradise. Adjacent to the lake, Raja and Safina stopped to rest.

"Hungry?" Raja asked.

Safina nodded.

"Go over there and sit by the lake – wait for my return."

"If I'm crazy enough to come this far with you on an empty stomach, a few short hours of wait should not hurt," she yelled back.

He smiled and he left Safina there, alone. People's King, that's what everyone called him who left her to deal with her own nemesis.

A couple of hours passed and yet there was still no sign of him. Clouds gathered in the meantime over the mountains and the lake changed from green to tinged grey. The passing of time had an effect on Safina, too. Her eyes stung, and she felt a slight obstruction in her lungs. Then she heard children's voices through the mist on the mountain pass. She looked in the direction of the sound, and there he was, her King with a group of children following him. He came down the slope, the children in tow to the lowland below.

"These are mountain orphans from the Circle of Cloudy Tops."

"Oh, I see. Is this who you give the money to?"

"Yes, to the borborygmi you hear in your belly, they hear it all year round."

"Do they not get enough to eat?"

"I cannot give them money directly, but to the paymasters, who then give them the bread crumbs that fall off the tables."

"Why?" Safina asked.

"Greed, what do you think? They steal food from the children," he said.

They were both sombre and looked at the children. They laughed and started to chant. They sat down on the dust in their wild, tattered pants. And then they began to sing a song. They sang a circle of fifths, some in minor and some in major keys starting at the point of C, in the sequence of C, G, D, A, E, B, F♯, C♯, A ♭ , E ♭ , B ♭ , F.

A creature appeared out of the grey lake, shaped like the highlander Nessie. It joined in the chorus and played its part in the music of the glen; the Nessie lookalike reared its long head, tail, and a black, distinctive hump. The vibration shook the heavens and the earth. Its mysterious ways eluded Safina, who stared at this spectacle, which was nothing short of divine sighting. It whipped up a storm which created huge waves, the colour of the lake changing from green to grey. The dust from the storm blinded Safina. She blinked for a second.

When she opened her eyes again, she noticed the quiet. Nessie was gone, and so was the storm. She gazed at the space without Raja or the singing. She saw nothing but the mountain range, the lake was turned back into green. The orphans stopped singing it but the melody wasn't lost. It ended up in the scroll as it were. The famished children vanished in the mist.

Safina's last link to the King was severed many Ramadans

197

ago. Raja did not dote on the merchants of the Silk Road, although their caravans came and went in a row. In all the world, the one desire Safina ever cherished was to be with her Raja and listen to the children's chants of the circle of the fifths.

But wait. The cosmic spirit of the azaan, kindred to its magic melody is as integral as the fairies are to the woodlands. It's never gone; neither is the circle of the fifths, nor the Sehri singing of Qasida singers on pale mornings. Safina and Rifaat, a one-bodied sprite, Raja and the children, must meet in infinite tune, wherein exists an unbreakable circle of all – space, time, and chime.

_____

First published by *Alien Buddha Press*, USA, May 2024

About the Author

Since childhood, Mehreen Ahmed has been inclined to read literary fiction. She read both in English and Bengali. Bronte's *Jane Eyre* (abridged) and Enid Blyton were a few childhood English books she loved. As an adult, and to name a few, she read and enjoyed Woolf's *Mrs Dalloway*, Tagore's *Shesher Kobita* – a Bengali classic, *Silent House* by Orhan Pamuk. Such readings perhaps inspired her to become a writer later, because earlier on she didn't write much apart from a personal diary. She began to take writing more seriously when she married and moved to Australia. However, her well-versed parents, and the voracious readers she grew up with influenced her in her formative years.

She has an MA in English Literature from Dhaka University, Bangladesh, and an MA in Computer Assisted Language Learning (Linguistics) from Queensland University, Australia. She has published ten books and over two hundred short stories in various literary magazines/ anthologies with nominations for the prestigious Pushcart/Best of the Net Awards. She has also written some academic articles.

Mehreen's undiminished love for literary fiction continues through her many reads, and she has just finished reading Mikhail Bulgakov's *Master and Margarita*. She still publishes her stories in various literary magazines such as CaféLit, Visual Verse, Litro, UK, and others. Gearing up for her next novel, she believes in the transformative power of the mighty sword, the pen.

She lives in Brisbane with her loving husband and wonderful children – a son, a daughter, and a son-in-law, whom she adores.

Acknowledgements

I would like to thank The Waterloo Writing Competition Festival, 2020 for selecting my short story, *Dolly*, included in this collection. *Dolly* also appears in *Transforming Communities* for all the winning stories in The Waterloo Writing Competition held in 2020, published by Bridge House Publishing. Thank you also for the selection of *Of the Blue Evening* as the best of 2023 Reader Favourite by The Gorko Gazette; *River of Melted Chocolate* by Alien Buddha Zine #52, *In Stillness, Space*, and *City Smell* as the best of Mad Swirl. *Perforation* is top 10 read on Impspired Magazine.

Additionally, I would like to thank Umair Mirxa Editor-in-Chief for Paper Djinn (folded) for nominating *Ylem* for the Pushcart Award 2020, and John Caulton Editor-in-Chief, of Flash Fiction North for nominating *Elysium* 2020, Literati Magazine Editors for nominating, *Interlude* 2020, Audrey Shipp Editor-in-Chief of Decolonial Passage for nominating *Number Ninety-four* 2023/24 for The Best of The Net Anthology Awards.

Pink Toenails, which appeared in my first collection, *Gatherings*, also published by Bridge House, has been included here as well. The rationale for this inclusion is this those who have not read *Gatherings* but have picked up *White Moon* by chance will be able to access this wonderful futuristic science fiction. When I was writing this story, AI or ChatGPT weren't as pervasive as it is today, and this story is uncannily reflective of that reality. Hence, *Pink Toenails* exists to be told and retold for broader readership, not get side-lined.

Like to Read More Work Like This?

Then sign up to our mailing list and download our free collection of short stories, *Magnetism*. Sign up now to receive this free e-book and also to find out about all of our new publications and offers.

Sign up here:
    http://eepurl.com/gbpdVz

Please Leave a Review

Reviews are so important to writers. Please take the time to review this book. A couple of lines is fine.

Reviews help the book to become more visible to buyers. Retailers will promote books with multiple reviews.

This in turn helps us to sell more books… And then we can afford to publish more books like this one.

Leaving a review is very easy.

Go to https://amzn.to/40sFcFy, scroll down the left-hand side of the Amazon page and click on the "Write a customer review" button.

Other Writing by Mehreen Ahmed

Incandescence
Published by impspired

Incandescence is a book about a fallen aristocratic family set in 1970, Bangladesh. In a nuanced tale of love and betrayal, the protagonist is on an introspective journey of the self, space, and time. Growing up in this odd and dysfunctional family, Mila Chowdhury discovers life's intrinsic value. That there is a huge gap between what is and what should be. How does one overcome such limitations and shortcomings? Paradoxically, the answer lay right here, within her own odd family.

"Incandescence is absorbing throughout and is an illuminating glimpse into a rich and exotic culture adapting painfully to changing times" (*Amazon*)

Order from Amazon:

Paperback: ISBN 978-1-915819-04-8

The Pacifist
Published by Cosmic Teapot

In 1866, Peter Baxter's misfortune ends the day he leaves Badgerys Creek orphanage. Unsure of what to do next, Peter finds himself on a farm run by Mr Brown. An aging man, Brown needs help and is happy to give Peter a place to live in exchange for his labor. Unbeknownst to Peter, Brown's past is riddled with dark secrets tied to the same orphanage, which he has documented in a red folder.

During a chance encounter, Peter meets Rose. Peter cannot help but fall in love with her beauty, grace, and wit; however, he fears that his affection will go unrequited as a result of his crippling poverty. But fate changes when Peter joins the search for gold in Hill End, New South Wales. Striking it rich, he returns to Rose a wealthy man. Peter is changed by his new found affluence, heading towards the mire of greed. Will Rose regret her relationship with Peter?

Meanwhile, Rose has her own troubled history. One that is deeply entwined with Brown's past and Peter's future.

"An Australian masterpiece" (*Amazon*)

Order from Amazon:

Hardrback: ISBN 978-1-988762-03-6
Paperback: ISBN 978-1-988762-06-7
eBook: ASIN B06XYRRZVW

Gatherings
Published by Bridge House

A collection of character based stories, some with a strong element of stream-of-consciousness style.

This book contains twenty-five unthemed short stories. The narratives are picturesque, evocative, and entertaining. They will take the readers on a journey laced with slightly amoral leanings to the serious and in-depth observations of the human condition. With both tragic and comic endings, vices and virtues, entwined into the hearts of the stories, they are all about ordinary people with mundane aspirations, broken dreams, and success.

Gatherings is a single author collection from Bridge House Publishing. Mehreen Ahmed has a well-established voice and is an experienced literary writer.

Order from Amazon:

Paperback: ISBN 978-1-914199-02-8
eBook: ISBN 978-1-914199-03-5

Other Publications by Bridge House

Butterflies
by Jenny Palmer

Imaginative, witty, topical stories with unexpected twists and turns.

The book portrays snippets of everyday life which contain a deeper meaning than is immediately apparent. There are stories about women who try to prove they are not invisible, people escaping from a cult, coincidental encounters with long lost friends, historical characters who reassert themselves into the present, scenarios which foreshadow what is to come, the danger of relying on other people's philosophy rather than one's own, along-side suggestions on how best to survive Christmas or deal with unwanted intruders.

"A wonderful collection of interesting tales. A real mixture that will delight all readers." *(Amazon)*

Order from Amazon:

Paperback: ISBN 978-1-914199-54-7
eBook: ISBN 978-1-914199-55-4

Feel-Good Stories
by Sarah Swatridge

A book to enhance your wellbeing and tug at your emotions.

An eclectic mix of heart-warming stories, full of memorable and quirky characters. Read about the heroic postie, the eccentric duke, a spoilt parrot, a true friend and a determined would-be husband. Perfect bite-sized reading with your favourite drink.

Enjoy Sarah Swatridge's uplifting *Feel-Good Stories*.

"A heart warming collection of short stories that do as the title suggests - make you feel good!" (Amazon)

Order from Amazon:

Paperback: ISBN 978-1-914199-62-2
eBook: ISBN 978-1-914199-63-9

www.ingramcontent.com/pod-product-compliance
Lightning Source LLC
Chambersburg PA
CBHW072102170626
46813CB00004B/1430